# THE MONUMENTS MEN MURDERS

Despite having attracted the attention of a stalker,
Special Agent Jason West is doing his best
to keep his mind on his job and off his own troubles.

But his latest case implicates
one of the original Monuments Men
in the theft and perhaps destruction of part
of the world's cultural heritage—a lost Vermeer.
But Naval Reserve Lt. Commander Emerson Harley
wasn't just a World War II hero—
he was the grandfather Jason grew up idolizing.
In fact, Grandpa Harley was a large part of what
inspired Jason to join the FBI's Art Crime Team.

Learning that his grandfather might have turned
a blind eye to American GIs "liberating"
priceless art treasures at the end of the war
is more than disturbing. It's devastating.

Jason is determined to clear his grandfather's name,
even if that means putting him on a collision course
with romantic partner BAU Chief Sam Kennedy.

Meanwhile, someone in the shadows
is biding his time…

# The
# MONUMENTS
# MEN
# MURDERS

## ART OF MURDER BOOK IV

*Josh Lanyon*

**VELLICHOR BOOKS**

*An imprint of JustJoshin Publishing, Inc.*

**The Monuments Men Murders**

**The Art of Murder Book IV**

June 2019

Copyright (c) 2019 by Josh Lanyon

Cover by Johanna Ollila
Book designed by Kevin Burton Smith.

Editing by Keren Reed

ISBN: 978-1-945802-47-8

Published in the United States of America
JustJoshin Publishing, Inc.
3053 Rancho Vista Blvd.
Suite 116
Palmdale, CA 93551
www.joshlanyon.com

*This is a work of fiction. Any resemblance to persons living or dead is entirely coincidental.*

*To Susan. And if you don't know why, you should*

# CHAPTER ONE

Fear was tiring.

Anger was preferable.

They were both draining.

Not that he was afraid all the time—most days he was too busy to really think about whether he was in danger, but sometimes at night, yes. Less so when he was away from home sweet home, which was ironic.

For a minute or two Special Agent Jason West of the FBI's Art Crime Team lay motionless, eyes probing the gloom of his Bozwin Montana hotel room, absently listening to—classifying—the nearby ice machine dumping its load, the gunning of a flooded engine in the parking lot, the clicking over of one luminous number in the clock on the nightstand.

3:43.

Make that 3:44.

He could always phone Sam. Even if by some chance Behavior Analysis Unit Chief Sam Kennedy was asleep, he'd take Jason's call.

Most likely he was awake.

Though Sam was halfway across the country, the thought of him comforted Jason. He could picture Sam, the glow from his computer monitor highlighting his craggy, not-quite-handsome face. Broad shoulders and hard, taut muscles beneath one of those severely tailored white shirts. At this time of night it would be unbuttoned, his shirtsleeves rolled up. He'd be wearing the gold-wire glasses Jason found peculiarly sexy and that distant, meditative look as he read over the day's bad news.

Tomorrow Sam would be in Montana.

Tomorrow they'd be together for the first time in three weeks. They'd met for a spontaneous (on Jason's part) and very brief Memorial Day get-together. Before that it had been eight weeks since they'd been in the same room together.

Long-distance relationships were never easy, and this one had more challenges than most. Still, it was better than the alternative. They had come painfully close to the alternative too many times to take it lightly.

If Sam was asleep, he needed the rest, and Jason resisted the longing to hear his voice for a few minutes. He had already called him once this week. He didn't want Sam thinking the strain was getting to him.

But yeah, of course the strain was getting to him.

Not during the day, not while he was working.

But Dr. Jeremy Kyser had the key to Jason's dreams, and more evenings than not, he opened the door to Jason's subconscious and strolled right in. Mostly, it was just a lurking sense of unease, worry. Jason spent a lot of dreamtime looking for Kyser's lost case file or a missing-person report; it didn't take a shrink to interpret any of that.

Other nights—like this one—Jason relived some version of his narrow escape from attempted abduction, and woke drenched in perspiration and gulping for air like a landed fish.

The details of the assault remained sketchy in his memory, so he was never sure which, if any, of his nightmares offered a true version of events. He just knew he woke scared and angry, and no end to it in sight.

He reached for the remote control on the bed stand and turned on the television. Late-night TV was his new best friend. There was some crazy old black and white movie on—something to do with a stage magician having marital problems—and Jason folded his arms more comfortably behind his head and settled in, prepared to occupy himself for a few sleepless hours.

The movie, *Eternally Yours*, reminded Jason of the last time he and Sam had worked together. Well, they had not really been working together. Jason had been recuperating from injuries sustained fighting off Kyser, and Sam had been determined to oversee the process.

Anyway, his memories of the stay with Sam's mother were good, the movie was pleasantly goofy, and he was content with the way the case had turned out in Wyoming. By the time the Cheyenne Resident Agency had managed to get their search warrants, the magician community of Laramie County had pulled off their own Top Hat White Rabbit. And maybe that was the way it was supposed to go.

Sam did not agree with Jason's thinking on that score, and it was a given he would not approve of what Jason was hoping to accomplish in Montana. Which was why Jason was planning to get this case wrapped up without ever having to ad—

His cell phone vibrated into life—and Jason vibrated with it. He was immediately aggravated with his jump. He swore, grabbed the phone, growled, "West."

"Agent West," Sam said smoothly. His voice was deep, softened around the edges by a hint of Western drawl. "Did I wake you?"

Somewhere along the line, "West," used when they were on their own, had become kind of a pet name.

Jason relaxed into the pillows. "No. I was just thinking about you."

"Ah."

"You might have felt a tingle at the base of your spine."

Sam's laugh was quiet, intimate. "You're in a playful mood."

"I am, yeah. Looking forward to tomorrow night."

"Me too."

Jason closed his eyes for a moment, grateful. There had been a time he wouldn't have dared take it for granted that if he and Kennedy were sharing air space, they'd be together every possible moment.

Sam sipped something on the other end. Jason smiled faintly, waiting.

Sam asked thoughtfully, "You want to talk?"

Jason admitted, "Not really."

"You want to listen?"

"Yeah. I want to listen to you talk dirty to me." He was kidding, of course, but not entirely. No point pretending he wouldn't like the relief and relaxation that came from sex. Any kind of sex. Sam was not much for dirty talk, especially over the airwaves, but it didn't hurt to ask.

Sam sipped his drink, considered, said gravely, "Are you touching yourself?"

Jason gulped a laugh, shoved the tent of his boxers down—ouch—*caution: men at work*—closed his hand around his cock. "Yeah. I am. I wish it was your hand wrapped around my dick."

He nearly laughed again—unsteadily—at the reflective silence that followed. Maybe Sam had gone to fix himself a snack. A strangled sound escaped him at that thought.

Sam said suddenly, softly, "I love fucking you. And I love making love to you. And I love that it's always both things when I'm with you."

Jason swiped the pad of his thumb across the head of his cock to get a little slickness to ease the dragging grip of his fist as he slid his hand up the rigid pole of his erection.

"I love you too," he said huskily.

Sam, sounding more like he was aiming for accuracy of information rather than seduction, said, "It's always good with you. It's always natural. It always feels right."

Jason bit his lip, and pumped himself. This was awkward and sweet and funny as hell, but if he laughed, Sam was liable to think Jason was laughing at *him*, and the fact was, Jason was laughing at himself and the whole situation and the fact that with all its limitations, this relationship meant everything to him.

Sam said, "And I like that you're trying not to laugh nearly as much as I like your laugh."

*So. Boom! Take that, West.* As usual, Sam was two steps ahead.

Jason moaned, providing sound effects, but also because that wild *snap*, *crackle*, and *pop* was starting to zing its way from his balls to his brain while ricocheting down every imaginable detour along the way.

The cell phone lying on the pillow beside his head slid down to his shoulder, so he missed whatever Sam said next. He gave himself a couple more efficient, perfectly timed strokes—imagining himself with Sam tomorrow night—and that vise-like hold of fierce tension erupted into exquisite relief.

He gasped, swallowed the rest of the sounds threatening to tear out of him, because his partner, Special Agent J.J. Russell, was in the room next door, and let the release wash through him in shuddery waves of pleasure.

Somewhere from the region of his shoulder blade, Sam said, "And yeah, I do love you, West."

When Jason had his voice back, he asked, "When does your flight get in?" He knew the answer to that. He just wanted confirmation nothing had changed. He was looking forward to this so much. Too much.

"I should be in the office by noon."

"Okay. I'll see you there at some point."

"Yes, you will. So save the last dance for me."

Jason grinned into the darkness. On the flickering television screen, David Niven had just managed the ultimate feat of magic by saving his marriage.

"Safe travels," Jason said. He did not want to hang up. Did not want to sever this tenuous connection.

Sam answered, "Sweet dreams, West."

* * * * *

"Hey, isn't that Martinez?" J.J. asked.

They were having breakfast in a restaurant not far from the Holiday Inn while waiting for their complainant, a Dutch investigator specializing in stolen art. The plan was to compare notes before heading out to interview Bert Thompson. Thompson, who ran a dude ranch in the next county, was the nephew of the recently deceased Roy Thompson, prime suspect in the theft of priceless art treasures during the final days of World War II.

"Hm?" Jason looked up from his coffee mug. Another cup and he might feel almost human. Or at least awake. His sleepless nights were catching up to him—although last night there had been a bright side to the insomnia.

He followed J.J.'s gaze to the café's hostess stand, where a man and woman dressed in that particular brand of budget-conscious business attire that proclaimed *law-enforcement officers!* waited to be seated.

Jason's mind was mostly on the upcoming meet with Hans de Haan, their contact. He vaguely remembered being introduced to Special Agent Martinez at the Bozwin resident agency the previous afternoon. She was a petite woman, probably early thirties, with very short dark hair and big brown eyes. Certainly attractive, though not J.J.'s usual type. Typically, Jason's partner went for statuesque blondes whose life ambition was a full page in *Sports Illustrated Swimsuit Issue*.

"Is it?"

"Yeah." J.J. slid out of the booth. "I'll ask them to join us."

He didn't wait for Jason's reply, leaving the table and going to greet the newcomers.

Jason mentally sighed. Technically, J.J. was still a first office agent. Not probationary, but still pretty green—although he'd had one hell of a first year, even excluding the time partnered with Jason. They'd been paired since February. Four long months. At first, Jason had been sure one of them was going to end the year in jail on homicide charges, but they had eventually settled into a functional and not unfriendly partnership. They were very different personality types, and J.J. believed his talents were wasted by his being shackled to the LA Field Office's Art Crime Team agent—and Jason wholeheartedly agreed, though for different reasons.

He lifted a hand in greeting when the two agents looked over at the table.

J.J. ushered Martinez and her partner through the crowded dining room. Jason rose. Martinez, smelling of Vera Wang (which Jason's sister Sophie wore) slid into the empty booth, her partner slid in beside her, and Jason waited so that J.J. could position himself across from his quarry.

The male agent, who introduced himself as SA Travis Petty, looked to Jason to be a bit younger than him, tall, blond, and muscular. He could have commanded his own *SI* layout.

"Good to meet you, West," he said. And then, "You were with Sam Kennedy in Massachusetts."

Jason studied him. "I was."

Yes, Petty was very good-looking. Blue eyes, square jaw, boyish thatch of springy light hair. As a matter of fact, he looked like a 1950s poster boy for the manly-occupation-of-your-choice.

Petty's smile was white and rueful. "What an opportunity. To work with Sam on his last case as a field agent."

"It was a learning experience."

Not *BAU Chief Kennedy*, but *Sam Kennedy*. In fact, just plain old *Sam*, which, given Sam's general reputation in field offices and resident agencies, seemed to imply an unexpected social connection. Or, at the very least, an out of the ordinary interest in the legendary BAU Chief.

"I was part of the Deerlodge Destroyer task force he headed two years ago. It was really enlightening."

"I bet," Jason said.

The disturbing case Petty was referring to was why Sam happened to be in Montana at the same time as Jason. The capture of a serial killer who had been using the Beaverhead-Deerlodge National Forest as his personal hunting ground had been one of Sam's final field assignments and, being Sam, he was following it to its final conclusion, helping the local team finalize their court case. Delegation was not and had never been his default setting.

"You're also Art Crime Team?" Martinez asked J.J. She had a pretty smile, but then tall, dark, and handsome Russell brought out the pretty smiles in women, young and old.

"God no."

Jason said, "It's more of a hostage situation in Russell's case," and the others—including Russell—laughed.

"He thinks he's kidding," Russell said.

"Yeah, no I don't."

Petty said, "I can tell you one thing, if there's ever an opening on his team, I'm going for it."

Jason smiled politely. Back to Sam, because no way was Petty talking about signing on with Jason or the ACT. It was doubtful he even registered on Petty's consciousness beyond being someone who had spent significant time with Sam.

He glanced at Martinez, who was eyeing her partner with affectionate resignation.

J.J. said, "You know, you're talking to Kennedy's BFF."

BFF could have meant exactly that—best buds—but Martinez's instant, "*Oh*," indicated she'd interpreted correctly. As did Petty, given his almost comical change of expression.

Jason directed a look at J.J., who said, "Hey, it's the truth."

Petty's mouth curved, but that was as far as the smile went. "Lucky you," he said.

# CHAPTER TWO

Awkward as hell.

Jason had never imagined Sam was a monk—nor that he was the first field agent Sam had propositioned—but for some reason, he hadn't anticipated ever running into one of Sam's sexual partners. Or at least, not recognizing the situation if he did. This Awkward Moment meme was all due to the coincidence of Sam's schedule for once syncing with his own.

The weird thing was, Petty wasn't even Sam's type. Sam's type ran to, well, Jason's type. Tall, lanky, dark-haired guys with high cheekbones and angular jaws. Guys who looked like Ethan. He found himself disconcerted that Sam had strayed from pattern, though he wasn't sure why it made him uneasy.

As the blue-uniformed waitress approached, Martinez said, "We really ought to get going. We were just going to grab something quick."

"You haven't even ordered yet," protested J.J., supremely oblivious to the undercurrents at the table.

The restaurant door opened with a *whoosh* of summery, dry Montana air, and a tall, thin man with sharp features, thinning dark hair, and a pointed beard entered. He looked around inquiringly.

"Here's our guy," Jason said. He glanced at J.J. "Why don't you go ahead and finish your breakfast. I'll fill you in on the drive."

J.J. gave him a look of gratitude, and Jason nodded his farewell to Martinez and Petty, slid out of the booth, and went to meet Dutch investigator Hans de Haan.

"Agent West?" De Haan recognized him before Jason reached him. De Haan's lean, ascetic face brightened. Behind round spectacles that emphasized his vaguely stork-like appearance, his shiny dark eyes warmed. "Thank you for everything you've done."

Jason shook his hand. "It's great to finally meet you, Mr. de Haan. You've done incredible work on this case." He meant that. He had the greatest respect for de Haan despite the can of worms de Haan's investigation had opened up for him personally.

He asked about de Haan's trip as they managed to squeeze in at the lunch counter.

Once they got the niceties out of the way, de Haan said, "Mr. Thompson is still refusing to speak to me. He says I must speak to Quilletta."

Quilletta McCoy was Bert's sister. There was a great-niece as well, but Bert and Quilletta were Roy Thompson's primary heirs. To them had gone all Roy's worldly possessions, including his spoils of war. In that idiosyncratic cache of stolen art and artifacts was the tantalizing possibility of a missing legendary Vermeer painting known as *A Gentleman Washing His Hands in a Perspectival Room with Figures, Artful and Rare*, last listed in a Dutch auction catalog in 1696.

The possibility of the Vermeer was what most excited—and worried—Jason. A rediscovered Vermeer was always going to attract a huge amount of media attention. And attention of any kind was the last thing he wanted. For a lot of reasons.

"Don't worry, we'll speak to Quilletta," Jason said. "And Thompson is sure as hell going to speak to me."

"I like your certainty, Agent West."

Jason shrugged. He had experience in convincing people it was in their best interests to talk to him.

"Not everyone in your government has been so cooperative."

No surprise there.

Jason said, "Regardless, there's no excuse for what Captain Thompson did—it reflects on his unit and the entire US occupying force."

"This is how I view it. The man was a thief. His is a family of thieves."

Well… It wasn't quite that simple. Thompson's heirs believed they had a legitimate and legal claim to items that had been in their family for over seventy years. And they weren't alone in thinking that.

Jason said, "At least Captain Thompson was there, at least he served. He'd seen combat. He'd seen…maybe too much. His motives could have been mixed. His family…they don't necessarily understand that they're attempting to hang on to stolen art."

"Not just stolen art—the cultural treasures of another country!"

True. But Jason wished de Haan could be a little less passionate about it. Or at least keep his voice down.

According to de Haan's painstaking research at the National Archives in Maryland, in 1945, Captain Roy Thompson had been part of the US occupying forces in the southwest region of Bavaria, where a treasure trove of art and cultural artifacts stolen by the Nazis had been discovered in the tunnels beneath a castle.

Jason didn't doubt de Haan's research—or deductions.

The problem he had was with Captain Thompson's claim that he had been allowed to remove the items by a commanding officer, one Emerson Harley.

Problematic because Harley had been one of the legendary Monuments Men, whose mission was the "Protection and Salvage of Artistic and Historic Monuments in War Areas." In fact, Harley had been Deputy Chief of the Monuments, Fine Arts, and Archives program.

Doubly problematic because Harley was Jason's grandfather.

Not just his grandfather, but his boyhood idol. It was because of Emerson Harley's courageous efforts to preserve and protect the world's cultural heritage that Jason had taken his love of art and passion for history and joined the FBI's Art Crime Team.

Hearing that Harley had not only turned a blind eye to what amounted to theft and looting, but had possibly been complicit was horrifying.

Not that Jason believed it. The idea was preposterous. But that didn't mean Grandpa Harley—or at least his good name—was unassailable. If mud was thrown, some of it would stick. That was inevitable, unless the accusations were nullified before they could ever be cast.

Emerson Harley had passed away four years ago and could not defend his name. Thompson had died one year ago and was also unavailable for questioning. Jason's only potential witnesses were the remaining Thompson family members. And regarding the provenance of the stolen art, the Thompsons currently denied having the items in question in their possession—while simultaneously trying to establish their legal claim to those "liberated" pieces they had already tried to sell.

"I understand. We're going to do everything we can to fix this."

De Haan smiled faintly. "You're still young enough to be idealistic, Agent West."

Jason smiled too. "You seem pretty idealistic yourself, Mr. de Haan. I'm sure plenty of people told you at the start of your search that you were never going to find these pieces."

"That is more true than you are aware."

De Haan did not know of Jason's personal connection to the case. No one did. No one *could*, because if his personal connection was discovered, Jason would be off the investigation in nothing flat and it would be handed over to another agent. An agent who might be willing to accept how things first appeared on paper as fact, an agent who wouldn't be willing to keep digging and digging, because he—or she—hadn't had the advantage of actually knowing Emerson Harley.

In Jason's opinion, his lack of objectivity was a plus because he knew going in that there was no chance in hell his grandfather had turned a blind eye, let alone condoned, the theft of the world's cultural treasures. He knew there was more to the story. Knew he had to keep digging to get to the truth.

"You've already done the hard part," Jason said. "Now it's a matter of sifting through the conflicting accounts."

J.J. joined them. He patted his pocket, his smile smug. "Ready to roll?"

Jason shook his head, said, "This is my partner, Special Agent Russell. Special Agent Russell, meet Hans de Haan, the art historian and private investigator hired by the Aaldenberg van Apeldoorn Museum."

He was relieved when Russell said, "Right. I read your notes on the case." Not something you could ever take for granted with Russell, who was counting the minutes until he was reassigned.

They shook hands, and Jason said to de Haan, "Do you want to follow us out to the ranch?"

De Haan assented, and they left the restaurant together.

As J.J. started the rental sedan's engine, he announced over the blast of air conditioning, "I just had breakfast with the girl I'm going to marry."

"The *girl*?" Jason repeated. "Did you notice this girl lives a thousand miles away from you?"

"Yes. That's not going to be a problem. She's got to be dying to get out of Siberia."

"Oh boy," Jason murmured, programming the car's GPS.

"Hey, your pal Kennedy lives double that, and I don't see you complaining."

"I'm not the complaining type."

J.J. hooted with laughter and put the car into drive.

**B**ig Sky Guest Ranch offered day trips to nearby Yellowstone National Park, an abundance of hiking trails, sparkling mountain streams for fishing, and whitewater rafting excursions on the Yellowstone River.

"The absolute best in Western hospitality," the chirpy redhead manning the front desk assured the three of them. She wore a short black denim skirt, a gray T-shirt with black stars, and a brass replica sheriff's badge, which read: Big Sky Deputy.

Jason told her it all sounded wonderful. He and J.J. offered their own IDs, and Jason asked to speak to Bert Thompson.

The redhead's face fell, she buzzed Thompson, informed him the FBI was in the lobby, and then listened to him rant, casting apologetic looks at Jason and J.J. as she tried to muffle the speaker.

"…be damned…can go to hell…my tax dollars…"

De Haan, hovering impatiently behind them, muttered, "See? They will whitewall us."

Jason winked at him, said gravely to the receptionist, "Make sure Mr. Thompson understands we're perfectly happy to wait here until it's convenient for him to speak with us."

She cleared her throat, conveyed the message, and winced at the response.

"He's, um, under a lot of stress," she whispered to Jason.

Jason turned to J.J. "He's under a lot of stress."

"That's a shame. Do you have the Wi-Fi password?" J.J. asked her. "We might as well file some reports while we wait in your lobby."

"Great idea," Jason said. "I need to phone my contact at the Department of Health and Human Services."

Two minutes and twenty-eight seconds later, the Big Sky Trail Boss himself slammed out of an office down a long hallway and strode into the knotty-pine lobby.

"What part of *no comment* do you fellows not understand?" he demanded.

Jason had seen several photos of Roy Thompson, and his nephew resembled him—same short dark hair and keen dark eyes—though he was shorter, stockier, and quite a bit grayer than the Roy of the WWII photographs.

"The part where you confuse federal agents with the members of the press," Jason replied.

Thompson threw an anguished look at the circle of guests playing cards at a table in the lobby living room. "Do you mind taking this outside?"

"Not at all. After you," Jason said.

They followed Thompson out onto the broad wooden porch that wrapped around the building.

Thompson said to Jason, "I told you people you need to talk to Quilletta. I don't know what more you want from me. I don't know anything about stolen art."

"And yet it's your name listed right along with hers as co-defendant in the lawsuit filed by the Aaldenberg van Apeldoorn Museum."

Thompson stuck his chest out. "That lawsuit doesn't mean anything. A foreign museum can't sue an American citizen."

"*Au contraire*, pardner," Jason said. "Not to mention the fact that Uncle Sam is liable to get into the act very soon if somebody named Thompson doesn't start demonstrating willingness to cooperate."

J.J. put in helpfully, "My partner is talking about a potential indictment for 'conspiring to receive, possess, conceal, store, barter, sell, and dispose of stolen goods, and for receiving, possessing, concealing, storing, bartering, selling, and disposing of stolen goods.'"

"There's also the possibility of an IRS investigation."

"True," J.J. said.

De Haan broke in. "It's too late to pretend you are acting in good faith when you ended off negotiations with the museum for the van Eyck in order to sell to a private collector!"

Jason put his hand on de Haan's arm. He could feel the older man shaking with agitation. This was personal for de Haan. He had spent years tracking down the missing pieces to that castle in Bavaria, and then more years following the trail of each and every US soldier tasked with protecting the recovered treasure. To be confronted with this final, outrageous obstacle was liable to be his breaking point.

"This is blackmail," Thompson said. "You can't force me to answer your questions, federal agents or not."

"No. This is giving you one final chance to cooperate before we reach the point of no return," Jason said. "Nobody wants a big, messy, and very expensive lawsuit, including the US government."

"Don't give me that," Thompson said. "You people live for your lawsuits. Well, I'll tell you this for free. If Uncle Roy did take some souvenirs, it was just what everybody else was doing."

Proving that he did occasionally pay attention to Jason, J.J. said, "This isn't about a flag or a German helmet or a confiscated Lugar. These are priceless works of art that belong to everybody."

"Yes, *everybody*," Thompson said hotly. "Including *us*. You know what I don't understand? Why the US government would be trying so goddamned hard to give those things back to the country who started the war in the first place!"

"S-s-started the war!" de Haan began to stutter in outrage.

Jason had heard this line of argument before. He said patiently, "The van Eyck was originally stolen from a cathedral in Belgium. Most of the paintings and jewelry were looted by the Nazis from museums or Jewish families in the Netherlands. The Belgian and Dutch people have a right—a legal and moral right—to reclaim their property."

"They didn't rescue the property—the *alleged* property. American soldiers like my uncle did. The damned Dutch surrendered after one day."

De Haan turned purple and then white. Behind the spectacles, his mild eyes blazed into fury. "Two hundred thousand people in the Netherlands *died*—"

"Okay, wait a minute." Jason gave de Haan a warning look. "This isn't up for debate. Mr. Thompson, you can refuse to answer our questions, but the investigation will continue. Your unwillingness to cooperate will be noted and used against you—"

Thompson was not listening to him. Was not even looking at him. He stared past them. "What the hell?" he muttered.

Jason automatically glanced over his shoulder.

"Jesus Christ," Thompson exclaimed, striding to the edge of the porch. "Is he out of his goddamned mind?"

A disreputable-looking white pickup was barreling down the dirt road toward the ranch. Dust flew up in a cloud around the bouncing vehicle. A man in a red shirt and a cowboy hat hung halfway out the passenger-side window, holding what appeared to be an automatic rifle.

Jason reached for his weapon as J.J. said, "Is that what I fucking think it is?"

Yes, it fucking was.

As the white truck hurtled beneath the towering timber ranch gate entry sign, the cowboy in the truck opened fire.

# Chapter Three

Instinct—and training—kicked in.

"*Get down!*" Jason knocked de Haan to the floor of the porch, aware of J.J. leaping left.

Bullets laced across the log cabin exterior, shattering glass and sending white wood chips and the stuffing from the cushions on chairs flying. From inside the building came screams and shouts of terror.

The automatic gunfire sent Jason's heart thundering in his chest, and blood roared in his ears. For a vital second or two, black edged across the corners of his vision. He desperately, *desperately*, did not want to be shot again.

"*Move,*" he urged de Haan, blindly pushing him to crawl to the end of the porch. De Haan didn't budge, his terrified gaze frozen on the swift-approaching truck. Jason spared a sideways look and saw the ranch house door slam behind Thompson. J.J., like him, was flattened to the planks of the porch, taking aim at the ever-larger target.

They were trained to handle this, but the surge of adrenaline was sickening. In a flash, Jason's fine muscle control was gone, his vision narrowed down to pinpoints: the sunlight glinting off the shooter's belt buckle, the tactical glasses the driver wore, the music blasting from inside the cab. *Music?*

Beneath the *tuttut-tuttut-tuttut* of automatic gunfire, "Old Town Road" floated on the dry, dusty breeze.

"Hans, *move*." Jason steadied his Glock and fired at the truck's right tire.

The tire went with a *bang*, the truck lurched, veered right, and the driver lost control. As the vehicle began to spin out, the shooter lost his balance and swung his assault rifle skyward, still firing. Bullets ripped through roof of the porch and the overhanging tree branches. The air smelled acrid, a sulfuric mix of engine oil and propellant and burnt wood.

Everything was happening at light speed, and yet somehow at the same time, in slow mo. Jason could hear J.J. swearing, hear de Haan praying, hear the people inside the building screaming and crying, hear his own quick, shallow breaths—which he immediately tried to slow and deepen. He took aim again.

J.J. fired and the shooter flew back, flung forward, and fell out of the careening truck. He hit the ground like a rag doll. The truck crashed into a tree and sent a wooden swing flying across the yard. Jason scrambled up, jumped over the railing, and ran toward the truck as the driver's door opened.

"Out of the vehicle with your hands on your head. Do it now!"

The driver, blood streaming down his face, locked his hands behind his head, staggered out from behind the door, knelt—and then pitched forward in a face-plant.

*"Can't nobody tell me nothin'..."* repeated the voice on the radio.

Jason reached the driver, weapon trained on the man's inert form, ready to shoot if the asshole so much as twitched.

He planted his knee in the guy's back, holstered his weapon, yanked one limp arm back and cuffed him, cuffed his other wrist, and rolled the driver over.

He was out cold.

He was also young. Early twenties. Wispy blond hair and an even wispier attempt at a beard.

Jesus Christ. Was this the Montana version of a drive-by?

"Russell?" he yelled.

"This fucker's dead," Russell shouted back. Like Jason, he sounded out of breath and pumped up on adrenaline.

"Hans?"

No answer.

Jason looked back in alarm.

Hans waved to him from the porch, clambered unsteadily to his feet. He dropped into one of the bullet-riddled chairs and put his face in his hands.

The door to the main ranch house flew open, and a mob of people poured out, everyone shouting and talking at once.

The Park County Sheriff's Office arrived before the FBI, but not by much. First on-scene was Bozwin Police Chief Amos Sandford.

Jason was unclear why the Bozwin chief of police had been summoned by Bert Thompson—Big Sky Guest Ranch was not even in the same county—but he was doing his best to cooperate.

Sandford reminded him a bit of a disgruntled polar bear. He was a big man. Tall, broad, and heavy. Not fat—not yet—but getting there. He had eyes the color of dirty ice and a head of longish silvery-white hair that furthered the impression of a dangerous arctic animal woken too early from hibernation.

He had been in the process of chewing out Jason and J.J. when the procession of government cars started down the long dirt road, and the sight of that cavalcade of shiny G-rides just made him louder and angrier.

"I want to know what the hell the FBI is doing traipsing around in my backyard without so much as a by-your-leave."

"I emailed your office twice," Jason replied. "And I phoned on Friday and spoke to your assistant chief, to let her know we'd be interviewing Bozwin residents."

"My assistant chief is not the one in charge."

"I couldn't get an answer from you."

"Then that was your answer!"

Jason was trying to keep his tone reasonable, but it wasn't easy after the morning he'd had, and he'd already gone through one round of questioning from the deputy sheriffs, who at least had a right to be on-scene.

"Sir, you don't have that option. Letting you know we were speaking to people in your community was merely a courtesy. This is a federal case. We have jurisdiction."

"Leave 'em the hell alone, Amos," Thompson suddenly chimed in. "Feds or not, these assholes saved my life. Not to mention the lives of several of my guests."

"The hell I will," Sandford snarled. He jabbed his finger at J.J. "This asshole killed someone in *my* backyard."

Abruptly, Jason lost his temper. "Backyard? This isn't even your county!"

"*I* decide what's in my county."

*Huh?*

That was a new one.

J.J., who had been uncharacteristically quiet through the butt-chewing, protested, "He was firing an automatic weapon at a house full of civilians!"

Sandford had opened his maw for another mauling, but that had been the moment the cavalry, or at least what looked like the entire staff of the FBI's Bozwin Resident Authority, had started taking up every available parking space not currently occupied by the sheriffs. There was something kind of solemn, even ominous, in all those official, unmarked vehicles silently filling the yard.

"Goddamn," Sandford muttered. "Why don't they send the black helicopters too?"

It did seem like a lot of agents for a tiny RA like Bozwin, but the reassembling of Sam's task force meant agents from Missoula and Helena had been in the office when the call came through, resulting in a pretty impressive show of force.

The Bureau preferred to handle agent-involved shootings in-house. That was what this was about.

Jason watched as a black SUV pulled up in front of the ranch house and Special Agent in Charge Elinor Phillips and her sole passenger got out.

Phillips was tall and athletic, with the kind of freckles that looked like a fashion statement rather than genetics. She wore a black pantsuit, and her champagne-colored hair was pulled up in a bun that bore zero resemblance to the version sported by schoolmarms and spinster cat ladies.

"Chief Sandford!" She sketched a wave to Sandford that might have been something else had sixty-plus people not been watching her. Despite the professional smile, Phillips didn't sound any more thrilled to see the police chief than he was to see her.

Jason glanced at the SUV's passenger. His heart jumped at the unexpected sight of Sam.

BAU Chief Sam Kennedy made an imposing figure in his favorite black suit, razor-sharp white shirt, and a black-cherry-colored tie. The summer breeze cheekily ruffled his pale hair, but behind the formidable dark glasses, Sam's face was steely.

His aftershave, an aggressive blend of musk and sandalwood, reached their enclave a couple of steps ahead of Sam—or Phillips.

"Problem?" He looked from Jason to Russell to Sandford.

Jason shrugged, nodded at Sandford. "Apparently there is, though I'm not sure why. It's not like we had a lot of options."

"What's going on, Amos?" Phillips questioned.

Sandford launched into a list of grievances. Support for Jason and J.J. came once again from Bert Thompson.

"My step-daughter's halfwit ex-boyfriend and his drooling moron cousin decided to shoot up the place. I guess Brody didn't believe my wife when she told him Patty wasn't here. Thank God she's with friends in Great Falls."

Sam gave Jason's shoulder a hard, reassuring squeeze. "You okay?" His blue gaze was searching—and assessing.

Jason nodded. He had stopped shaking, his heartbeat was normal again, but he still felt a little queasy, a little shaky. He would never admit it, but it was the truth. Reaction, plain and simple, and Sam probably knew it, because he gave Jason's shoulder another of those bruising grips.

Their relationship wasn't a secret, but it wasn't common knowledge either, although maybe that had changed since breakfast. Part of the expectation, though, was that on the job they could restrain themselves to treating each other like coworkers and not romantic partners. No dramatic clinches or *thank God you're all right, darling*.

Everything Sam was feeling had to be conveyed by a shoulder squeeze, and everything Jason felt had to be confined to even more briefly covering Sam's hand with his own.

Phillips's alert hazel gaze took note of the exchange. She said to Jason, "Then this is not related to your case?"

"This is nothing to do with our case. We just happened to be in the right place at the wrong time."

"The *right* time," de Haan objected. "These agents saved my life and the life of everyone on the ranch."

"And you are?" Phillips asked.

As de Haan began to explain who he was, they were joined by two detectives with the Park County Sheriff's Office. Sandford launched yet again into his complaints.

For Jason, time was of the essence, and it was painfully clear that his entire day was going to be lost to the fallout of this goddamned unfortuitous shooting. He did his best to control his frustration.

And the press hadn't even got wind of the incident yet.

He and J.J. were questioned separately by the sheriff's office detectives. It was pretty routine, and Jason could tell that the sheriffs—unlike Police Chief Sandford—were eager to hand this one off. Typically, law enforcement deferred agent-related shootings to the Bureau to investigate, but sometimes they chose to conduct their own investigation. Either way was fine by him. He was confident any shooting-incident inquiry was going to back up their decision to engage.

He just wanted the whole thing over so he could get on with his own investigation. The clock was ticking. Loudly. But he seemed to be the only person who could hear it.

SAC Phillips finally managed to appease Police Chief Sandford, who instructed Jason to inform him before he attempted to interview anyone in "his" town.

By that point Jason had had his fill of the overbearing asshole—which was saying something because he'd had a lot of experience with overbearing assholes.

"That is not going to happen," Jason told him.

Which nearly resulted in setting Sandford off again.

"Just simmer down," Sam told Sandford. He did not actually plant his hand in the center of Sandford's uniformed chest, but it had the same effect. Sandford rocked back as though he had been yanked by an invisible chain.

Rock meet hard place.

Sandford began to splutter. "You put a goddamned hand on me—"

Sam grinned. It was not a nice, friendly grin.

Sandford turned several shades of rage.

"OH-*kaaay*," Phillips interceded. She threw an exasperated look at Sam. "*No one* is putting a hand on anyone, *boys*. And Agent West will cooperate fully with the police department." Phillips's glance in Jason's direction was one of dire warning.

Jason said nothing. He did not need—and was not about to—coordinate his efforts with the Bozwin Police Department.

He had more pressing concerns than SAC Phillips's public-relations efforts.

After Sandford left the scene, Jason and J.J. were directed back to Bozwin and the RA, while Phillips's team and the sheriff's department finished up at the crime scene.

J.J. was silent for most of the nearly hour-long drive through scenic green-gold Paradise Valley. Beneath dramatic blue skies, vast and breathtaking views of the Absaroka Beartooth Mountains stretched to the east and the jagged snow-capped Gallatin Range dominated the west.

"You okay?" Jason asked J.J., surfacing from his own grim preoccupation.

"Sure," J.J. said tersely. "You?"

"Great."

They exchanged bleak looks.

"You don't have to worry," Jason said. "There's no way the SIRG won't find in your favor."

Typically, when an agent fired their weapon outside of a shooting range, the Bureau's Inspections Division sent out a Shooting Incident Review Team. The SIRT would interview witnesses and use forensics to reconstruct events in order to file a report with the Shooting Incident Report Group. The SIRG, comprised of high-level FBI and Justice Department officials, would then review the findings and determine whether the shooting complied with the Bureau's policy on using lethal force.

"I know." J.J. was staring out the windshield. "I'm not worried."

Sure.

They had both shot to kill on Camden Island. The crucial difference was they had *not* killed. Today... Well, neither would forget today.

Jason said, "You didn't have a choice, J.J. It was a good shoot."

J.J. nodded.

As Jason feared, the rest of his afternoon went to dealing with the fallout from the shooting.

SAC David Warner flew in from the Salt Lake City field office with Brian Dulaney, one of his three Assistant Special Agents in Charge. An attorney from the Department of Justice arrived separately, followed by two representatives from the FBI Agents Association.

Jason and J.J. were again questioned apart and at length.

Most of it was basic, checking-off-boxes stuff. SAC David Warner asked Jason three times in three different ways why he had fired at the oncoming vehicle and not the shooter.

Jason wasn't completely sure himself, but he didn't admit that. "I thought the approaching truck posed the greater threat to more people—civilians—than just me and my partner."

"It was a reasoned and informed decision?" Dulaney inquired.

"It was gut instinct," Jason admitted. "I'm only thinking it through now."

Bozwin Supervisory Special Agent James Salazar asked, "Why do you think your partner chose to target the shooter?"

This was what they were really after. Had J.J. had a choice, or had he opted for a lethal resolution in a non-lethal situation?

Jason answered carefully, "I think Agent Russell perceived correctly that the shooter was the immediate threat and that he—Agent Russell—had the better line of sight. Which, as I consider, is another reason I went for the truck. I knew Russell would go for the shooter."

"Team work at its best?" SAC Phillips was neutral, but maybe a little skeptical. She had been pleasant enough when they'd met the day before, but this afternoon Jason had the distinct feeling she didn't much like him.

Jason answered, "We're trained to trust our partners."

On it went. The same questions reworked and reapplied. But eventually Jason was dismissed and J.J. was brought back in for another round.

Sam, of course, was not part of these interviews. When Jason stepped out to grab a late lunch, he had a quick look for Sam and spotted him through the windows of the conference room, sitting at a long table strewn with laptops, cell phones, and fast-food containers, speaking to a group of agents clearly hanging on his every word.

And no one was hanging tighter than Special Agent Travis Petty, sitting right there at the left hand of God, a.k.a. BAU Chief Sam Kennedy.

Late afternoon, Phillips summoned Jason to her office to inform him Warner was about to make a formal statement to the press.

"Okay. Sure." Jason was wondering uneasily whether Warner was about to surprise them with some unpleasant development. There was something odd in Phillips's expression.

Phillips said, "According to Unit Chief Kennedy, any media attention focused on you is undesirable, so I'm giving you a heads-up. We have a friendly relationship with the local papers, and there are liable to be reporters in the building. I'd stay in your office and keep the blinds down for the next couple of hours."

Right. In case the story was picked up by the national networks and Jeremy Kyser, everyone's favorite psycho stalker, happened to turn on the TV and see where Jason West was spending the next few days.

It was a little embarrassing—not least because he hadn't even thought of this potential threat—and he was a little angry too at the reminder of Jeremy Kyser out there and waiting. Even after two months of no sign of Kyser, a knot of nerves and tension instantly formed in his belly at the mere mention of his name.

He could see the curiosity in the back of Phillips's eyes.

"Thanks," Jason said, and retreated to the temporary office assigned to him and J.J. during their stay.

He spent the rest of the afternoon answering emails and talking with Supervisory Special Agent George Potts, his immediate boss at the LA Field Office.

"How do you think J.J. is handling the shooting?" George asked.

"I can't tell. Probably better than I would."

Of course, you weren't supposed to confess that, but George would understand. In his entire career, George had never fired his weapon off the shooting range.

"There's support here if he needs it. I've been talking to SAC Warner. Do you think it might be best to hand this case off to Salt Lake City's ACT? It's their backyard, after all."

Jason swallowed his instant alarm. "No. It's a complicated case. It would take Janelle too long to get up to speed. Time is of the essence. We don't want the family deciding to solve their legal problems by destroying the art they still deny having."

Sweat prickled his hairline and underarms as he waited for George's answer.

"Okay," George said at last, "but Warner says they've got the resources. And it's not like you don't have plenty of your own cases waiting back home."

"I know. But this case is too important to risk something getting lost in the handoff. And de Haan did come to the LA Office."

That was something of a miracle. De Haan had happened to read an article about Jason working with an LA County museum to make proper restitution to the heirs of a Nazi-looted van Gogh, which had hung on the museum's walls for over fifty years.

Historically—and still all too often—museums and galleries resisted restoring stolen art or even making a serious attempt at restitution, so the news story and Jason's role in it had stood out for de Haan.

George said reluctantly, "Well, I guess if you think your participation is vital to the successful resolution of the case…"

That made Jason sound like a complete egomaniac. But he not only had to stay part of the investigation, he had to be the one *directing* the investigation. He said, "I really do."

"Okay, Jason." George sounded more resigned than approving. "It's what the museum wants, and you've done the groundwork on this. I'll confirm our need to take point with Warner."

Jason felt giddy with relief. "Thanks, George. I promise I won't let this case linger one minute longer than it has to."

And that was the truth. No one had greater interest than him in seeing this thing wrapped up quietly and quickly.

It was after five, and Jason was just hanging up from his phone call with the chief of the Major Theft Unit of the Criminal Investigative Division, Karan Kapszukiewicz, when someone rapped on the door. Sam ducked his head into the office.

"Hey." Jason smiled welcome.

"Hey." Sam was not smiling. "Sorry about this." Sam kept his voice down. "I've got dinner with the task-force members tonight."

Of all the goddamned times. But disappointing though this was, it was not unexpected that Sam would be tied up for most of their evenings. There were always dinners out with the resident team, especially for someone in Sam's position. Jason kept his smile in place. "I figured." His gaze traveled to Travis Petty hovering behind Sam in the hallway. He nodded politely to Petty, who nodded politely back.

"I'll give you a call afterward?" Sam said still more quietly.

"Yeah. I'd like that."

A smile flickered across Sam's gaze, though the next instant he was his usual unreadable self.

He nodded curtly and closed the door to Jason's office.

# CHAPTER FOUR

It was nearly six by the time J.J. was finally finished being interviewed and the brass and legal reps headed out to catch their planes.

Jason had delayed leaving until he could speak with J.J. No, they weren't pals, but that's what you did when you were partners. There was no denying that fighting for your life shoulder to shoulder with a guy created a bond.

He couldn't read anything in J.J.'s expression beyond weariness, and he seemed to have nothing to report. "Ready to go?" he asked Jason.

"Sure. You want to grab some dinner?"

J.J. was swiftly gathering his things. "Nope. I've got a date."

"Who with?"

J.J. looked at him like Jason was an idiot. "With Martinez, of course."

Jason's surprise must have shown because J.J. scowled. "It's not going to help sitting around talking about it. I need to change the subject."

"No. Sure. I get it."

"Plus, I've only got another couple of days here. I'm not wasting this chance."

"Yeah, absolutely," Jason said. "Fine by me."

Was J.J. serious about Martinez? He'd never figured his partner for a love-at-first-sight kind of guy, but this was definitely not his usual MO.

"And if I were you, I wouldn't spend the night second-guessing yourself either."

About the shooting? No. Jason wasn't second-guessing his decisions that morning. Now that the initial shock had worn off, he was simply relieved he hadn't frozen and that neither he nor his partner nor anyone in their charge had been shot. About other things? Yes, his conversations with George and with Karan had reinforced his guilty awareness that he was sinking deeper and deeper into ethically murky waters.

Having made a point of insisting he was best qualified to pursue the investigation based on being fully versed in every aspect of the case—true, for the record—there was no way he could later claim he hadn't realized his personal connection.

He hated being in this position. The knowledge that he was risking a job he loved and a career he was proud of was an almost physical weight on his mind. He just didn't see a way around it.

"I appreciate the advice."

"No, you don't. But I'm right."

J.J. was still talking about the shooting. Still processing it. And he *was* right. There was nothing to be gained by reliving those terrifying seconds. They had not been shot. They had done their job and taken the necessary steps to protect civilians and property.

J.J. was the one who had to live with the consequences of that action, so if a night out with a fellow agent in a faraway RA was going to take his mind off it for a while, more power to him.

When they parted ways at their hotel, Jason said, "Have a good night."

J.J. answered, "Stay out of trouble."

* * * * *

"I still find it hard to believe the shooting had nothing to do with the treasure," de Haan said.

They were having dinner at the Club Tavern and Grill, a surprisingly cozy sports bar and restaurant offering an all-American menu and an outstanding selection of beers and booze.

Still wound up from the day's action, Jason had realized he didn't want to be alone, and he didn't want to spend the evening imagining Sam out with his task force—or more precisely, imagining Sam rubbing elbows with the handsome and admiring Travis Petty. He'd phoned de Haan, and de Haan had picked him up from his hotel.

"I know, but that does seem to be the case," Jason said. "Brody Stevens was mad at his ex-girlfriend and thought shooting up her parents' home and business would teach her a lesson."

"You Americans and your guns."

Jason sighed. Like most law-enforcement officers, he was not happy with every dumbass in the country having access to a personal arsenal, but this was not a conversation he wanted to have here and now.

De Haan put his Bozone Amber down. "When I saw that truck coming toward us, I felt certain…"

De Haan didn't finish it, and Jason eyed him curiously. "You believed there was some connection to Captain Thompson's trove of stolen art?"

"There is a lot of money involved," de Haan said. "People have killed for much less."

"Yes." That was certainly true. Two of the rediscovered paintings—d'Antonio's *The Siege of Veii* and Nolde's *Poppies and Roses*—would easily fetch a million dollars apiece. Jason said, "If the Vermeer really exists, well, if you figure *The Concert,* the Vermeer stolen in the Gardner Museum heist, would fetch over ten million if it ever reappeared and went up for auction. *Gentleman* would probably be worth…"

"Inestimable," de Haan murmured, and Jason couldn't argue.

He did say, as much to remind himself as de Haan, "The odds of Thompson's stolen painting actually being a Vermeer are pretty slim."

De Haan quoted, "'Untitled. Man washing his hands in a see-through room with sculptures and art.'"

Yes. That description was startlingly close to the listing in the Dissius catalog.

And yet, as the poets said, so far away.

"I wonder why it was untitled," Jason mused.

De Haan chuckled. "I think you are secretly an art historian, Jason."

"It's no secret," Jason said. "I have a master's in Art History."

"Ah! I see. But that explains your conscience about seeing these works returned to their rightful owners."

"Everyone on the ACT has that same conscience," Jason felt obliged to point out.

De Haan shrugged, unconvinced. "As for the painting, it only appears in the Dissius catalog, and that is twenty years after Vermeer's death. It would have likely come from the collection of his patron Pieter van Ruijven."

"Not necessarily. Maybe it was one of his last works," Jason said. "Maybe that's why it was untitled. It might even be unfinished."

"Titles were not Vermeer's strength," de Haan pointed out.

"True." Jason was silent as their meals arrived. "California" steak sandwich for de Haan and steak salad for him. It took effort to eat healthy on the road. These days it took effort to eat at all. When the waitress left with the promise of condiments and another round of drinks, Jason asked, "Have you ever imagined what the painting would look like?"

De Haan's face brightened. This kind of discussion was meat and drink to art historians. "Something like *The Love Letter*, I think. Vermeer experimented with the perspectival room at least twice, but *The Love Letter* was his best effort."

"He tried earlier with *A Maid Asleep*," Jason agreed. "But the use of the pictorial device is not as striking."

"*Doorkijkje.*"

"*Doorkijkje,*" Jason repeated, "is used a lot in Dutch painting of the period."

"It is, yes. You know what is *not* used in the genre painting of the era? What theme or image does *not* show up in a single Dutch painting? A gentleman washing his hands."

"Is that true? I had no idea."

"It's true. This painting is unusual for many reasons. Do you know it sold for 95 guilders at the auction? One of the highest-priced works of the auction."

"Yes. That I did know."

For a moment they sat in silence, both smiling a little at the idea.

De Haan seemed to come back to reality. He gave his head a little shake, once again reminding Jason of a stork—this time, a stork waking from a pleasant daydream. "I fear that Quilletta McCoy will not appear tomorrow."

On Tuesday they had a meeting scheduled for eleven in the morning with Captain Thompson's niece at her lawyer's office.

"I think she'll show," Jason said. "I think that's the reason we're meeting at her lawyer's."

"She has not kept her word so far."

That was unfortunately true. When the Aaldenberg van Apeldoorn Museum had got wind that the van Eyck had come on the market, the curator had attempted to strike a deal with the Thompsons. The Thompsons—or at least Quilletta—had ostensibly considered the museum's offer but ultimately decided to go with a higher bid from a private collector. *Nothing personal. Just business.* Except it *was* personal to the museum. Very personal. And so, a civil lawsuit had been filed and the FBI had been contacted.

That was when Jason learned that the family insisted they had a legal right to the art and artifacts brought home by Captain Thompson because he had been given permission to do so by the Deputy Chief of the MFAA. A man who happened to be very well known to Jason because he was the man who had taught Jason to swim, to fly-fish, to shoot, to shave, to tie a bow tie, and, most importantly, to appreciate art, history, and even civilization itself. No one had influenced and shaped Jason's life more than his Grandpa Harley.

He said now, "I know. I got the impression after speaking with Thompson today that they truly believed they couldn't be sued by a foreign entity. Now that the US government is involved and the FBI is knocking on their door, I think we'll see movement. We're not dealing with hardened criminals."

"If she fails to show up tomorrow, I'll go to her home and insist she speak to me."

"I strongly recommend you don't do that."

"I will not let these thieves get away with their crimes."

"I understand how you feel. I do. Please believe me, it'll go more smoothly tomorrow if you allow me to do the talking," Jason said.

De Haan scowled. He picked up his beer and sipped, his expression stubborn.

Jason said, "You have to remember Thompson's niece and nephew may not have known the history of these paintings and other items. It's more than plausible that they grew up seeing these things in their uncle's home, and believed they'd inherited family heirlooms."

De Haan began to object, and Jason said, "It's not going to hurt to give them the benefit of the doubt, right?"

"That remains to be seen. You can't stop me from trying to speak to her."

"No, I can't," Jason said. "But you don't have any authority to do so."

"It doesn't seem that you do either," de Haan retorted.

"I can't force her to answer my questions, no. But I do have means of putting legal pressure on both her and her brother. I don't want to go that route if we don't have to because there's always the danger that if they think they're trapped, they'll destroy the remaining works—assuming they have possession of them."

De Haan's hand shook. He set his mug down.

"Plus, anything you learn is liable to be ruled inadmissible in court, which will further complicate my efforts."

"They tried to sell the van Eyck altar piece even while pretending to negotiate with the Aaldenberg van Apeldoorn Museum," de Haan reminded him. "They can't be trusted."

"I'm not forgetting. And I'm not saying we take what they say as gospel. Just keep in mind that their willingness to sell these items shows they don't have any emotional attachment to them."

De Haan considered. His shoulders slumped. "I understand."

"I understand too," Jason said. "You've been working this case a long time."

"Nearly twenty years. Since I was a grad student hired by the museum board of directors to research what had become of these lost and stolen pieces."

"Even longer than I thought." It put into perspective Jason's efforts to nail Fletcher-Durrand.

"Yes. Almost half my lifetime. In fact, this search has been my life." He brooded for a moment. "Are you married, Jason?"

"No."

"But you have someone in your life?"

Jason smiled a little, thinking of Sam. "Yes."

"I have someone too. Her name is Anna. We've been together for five years."

Happily, de Haan seemed to have moved on from his idea of waylaying Quilletta McCoy with a surprise interrogation. "What does Anna do?"

"She teaches architecture at the Amsterdam School of Arts. What she would *like* to do is have a child. I promised her that when this case was concluded, we would do so."

"That's great. And it won't be too much longer now," Jason said. "Or at least your role is coming to an end." He felt compelled to warn, "The case could hang up in the courts."

"For years," agreed de Haan. "Almost certainly that is what will happen if we can't force the Thompsons to the bargains table."

"Bargains table is right. But we've still got a few cards up our sleeves," Jason reassured him.

De Haan seemed doubtful.

When they finished their meal, de Haan insisted on paying for dinner. "You saved my life today. It is the least I can do."

"That's my job," Jason said. "But it was also my pleasure."

De Haan said stubbornly, "This is my pleasure."

"Well, okay. Thank you."

They walked out into the summery evening—still light at nine thirty—and de Haan drove Jason back to his hotel and dropped him off.

Jason was hoping Sam's dinner would be winding up soon. He ordered a drink in the Dry Fly Saloon, the bar located in the hotel lobby, and was just finishing his third Kamikaze—they served them in cocktail glasses there—when Sam strolled in a little after eleven.

For a moment, Jason just enjoyed watching Sam unaware he was being observed.

Granted, in a way that was always Sam because Sam had zero concern in anyone observing or not observing him.

He was a big man. Big personality and big physical presence. Tall, shoulders like a warship, and long, muscular, runner's legs. He looked good in a suit and even better naked, although at forty-six, a little bit of softness, roundness, wouldn't have been unexpected. But nope, there was not one ounce of superfluous flesh on Sam Kennedy's body. He ran every day, rain or shine, boxed, lifted weights, and worked out regularly. He watched his diet, did not smoke, and only drank to excess on weekends—which he rarely took, so that was moot.

Maybe he was a little fanatical in the personal-upkeep department. That went with being a little fanatical about his mission. Mission being what most people referred to as a job.

Which Jason couldn't object to since his family and friends referred to *him* as a workaholic. In fact, that shared work…ethic? was probably one of the reasons they were able to maintain their long-distance relationship—if you wanted to call these long gaps of not seeing each other maintenance.

Anyway, it seemed to Jason that these days Sam was a little more...maybe not relaxed. But more at ease? He even smiled at the girl behind the reception desk. Okay, he didn't actually *smile*, but he did curve his cheek briefly.

*Happy.*

Was that the word? Was happy even in Sam's vocabulary? Not that he ever seemed unhappy. The whole concept of happiness seemed too flimsy to stand up to the stainless-steel edges of Sam's psyche.

But yeah, if Sam were a mere mortal, Jason would have to say he did seem happier these days.

Jason's mouth quirked at the thought, he was still watching Sam, and Sam glanced over, spotted him—and smiled.

An actual smile this time. It lit his eyes, softened his face.

Jason's heart did a little flip.

Sam came across to him.

"Hi. Have you been waiting long?"

Jason shrugged. "Not really. How was dinner?"

"Prolonged." Sam studied him. "Did you want another drink?"

Jason considered. "Did you?"

"No."

Jason's smile widened. "Me neither."

# CHAPTER FIVE

"**A**ny word on our mutual friend?" Jason asked in the elevator as Sam loosened his tie.

If Sam had news, Jason would have heard it by now, but he still had to ask.

"No." Sam was terse because he didn't like having to admit failure. Even when the failure wasn't his.

Dr. Jeremy Kyser had disappeared, ostensibly after attending a conference in Toronto in April. Jason believed there was some question as to whether Kyser had ever been at the conference. He was convinced Kyser had sent a double in his place so that he could travel to Los Angeles. A card from Kyser had been hand-delivered to Jason's Venice Beach bungalow while Jason was recuperating in Wyoming.

But as Sam pointed out, there was no proof Kyser had not attended the conference himself. The card could have been delivered by someone in Kyser's pay or even a friend.

Did guys like Kyser have friends? Or were they more accurately called accomplices?

Since the macabre greeting card, there had been no further word from Kyser.

Which was good news, of course. As far as it went.

Which was never going to be far enough, in Jason's opinion.

Sam said, "There's an ongoing BOLO." He hesitated. "They're debating on whether to put him on the Most Wanted List."

Jason was aware of the debate, and he understood the reason for it. There was no actual evidence that Kyser was his assailant. There was no evidence Kyser had broken any law. There was not even an openly stated threat in the cards he had sent Jason. The only reason the idea was even being floated was because Jason was an FBI agent—and a politically connected one at that.

"Maybe he lost interest," Jason said.

A guy could hope.

Sam shook his head. "I don't think so. If he'd lost interest, he would not be in hiding."

"He has to know he's a suspect in the attempted abduction of an FBI agent."

"That information hasn't been released to the press."

"But—"

"Yes, he's aware he's under investigation, but that's only part of it. In my opinion, Kyser going into hiding indicates some kind of plan is in motion."

"Swell." Jason thought it over. "Maybe he's not hiding. Maybe he's dead."

A guy could hope for that too.

"Then his body would have turned up."

Jason resisted the urge to keep arguing. It sprang from the desire to talk away the threat. He would love to be able to convince himself the danger was not real and present.

Unfortunately, it was.

The elevator reached Sam's floor, and the doors opened with a *ding*.

Sam's room looked like Jason's. Same neutral palette color scheme, same buy-it-by-the-bushel artwork on the walls, same selection of nondescript furniture: desk with mirror, king-size bed, solitary "comfortable" chair, dresser with TV and coffee maker. A small balcony overlooked the tree-shaded parking lot and offered a view of the shadowy mountains. Sam's still-packed suitcase sat on the floor at the foot of the bed.

Sam tossed his key on the tray with the coffee mugs and packets of Sweet'n Low. He turned to Jason. "Hi."

Jason smiled into Sam's eyes. "Hi."

They kissed, warmly, unhurriedly, and Jason felt everything in him unclench and relax.

Sam kissed him again, said, "I've been wanting to do this since I saw you standing in that ranch yard this morning."

"Same." Jason grinned. "That would have raised a few brows."

"A few." Sam's blue gaze was penetrating. "You sure you're okay?"

"Yeah. Of course."

Sam studied him for a moment, deciding for himself. Jason must have passed his psych evaluation because Sam asked, "Russell okay?"

"I don't know. I don't think he's absorbed it yet."

Sam nodded, agreeing with that.

"The brass flew in from Salt Lake."

"Of course." Sam considered him. "You're not worried about the shooting review, are you?"

"No. It was a good shoot."

Sam said dryly, "Even if it wasn't, it's pretty rare the Bureau finds an agent at fault."

No kidding. In 228 shooting incidents ranging from 2011 to the present, the Bureau's internal review process had only five times found that agents acted improperly in discharging their weapons, and none of those times had been fatalities. Granted, there were very good reasons for that. Unlike a city police force, FBI agents tended to be older, better trained, more experienced, and maybe more to the point, not out there patrolling the streets and responding to in-progress crimes and unpredictable situations. When the Bureau went in, they went in with overwhelming force and a well-thought-out strategy.

"There was no gray area there," Jason said. "It was fight or die."

Sam said grimly, "It looked like it to me. And you agree the incident wasn't connected to your case?"

"Yes. I mean, yes, I agree, and that's what I believe. There doesn't seem to be much doubt the shooting wasn't connected. It's just really weird and random that we happened to be there today."

"Lucky for your subject."

"Yes."

"Were you able to interview him before hell broke loose?"

"Yes. Sort of. He was uncooperative." Not for the first time, Jason considered confiding in Sam. Sam knew the bare bones of the case, of course; what he did not know was that Captain Thompson had implicated Jason's grandfather in his theft of paintings and other items.

If Sam had known, in all likelihood he would have tried to convince Jason to recuse himself. That was certainly what Jason would recommend to another agent in his position.

Sam's hand arrowed down beneath Jason's belt, the waist-bands of his jeans and boxers. "You're losing weight, West."

Jason jumped at that caressing intrusion. He didn't bother to answer, raising his face to find Sam's mouth, kissing him.

Sam kissed him back, but he murmured, "I worry about you."

Jason shook his head. "Don't. I'm okay—and I'm not here for my biannual weigh-in."

Sam cocked an eyebrow. "No? What are you here for?"

Jason raised his eyes innocently heavenward as though trying to decide. "My biannual fuc—"

Kennedy laughed, withdrew his hand, and smacked Jason's ass.

Sam liked to make love with the lights on.

"I like to look at you," he said simply. "I like to look in your eyes, I like to see your face. You're very expressive, and that's...enjoyable."

Jason made a face—*see, very expressive!*—and laughed. He had no preferences beyond wanting to have sex with Sam as often as possible. Okay, he could have done without the uninspired floral pairing undoubtedly from the Propac Hospitality Images Collection viewed over Sam's shoulder. But all he really wanted to look at was Sam anyway.

That soft, almost boyish fall of blond hair across Sam's forehead—there was so little that was boyish about Sam—the crescent blue-black shadows of eyelashes on his hard, lean cheeks, the way his white teeth bit his lower lip as he thrust into Jason, and that hot, intense light in his blue eyes as he focused, unblinking on Jason's face.

Sam was usually quiet and intense during sex, but tonight he half groaned heartfelt, broken sentences. "So good...so beautiful...want...you...so...much..."

Jason gasped as the long strokes grew short and fierce, shoving back into it, riding the pleasurable surge and swell of relentless tide.

"*Ah...ah...ah...*" He was as loud in sex as Sam was usually terse. "Oh God... Oh God... Oh, Sam... *Jesus*, Sam...that. Oh God, do that again...*ahhh...*"

Every so often Sam would start laughing and cover Jason's mouth with his own, but not tonight. Tonight he was honed in and laser intent. Jason knew Sam had been afraid for him and was reacting from some deep, inarticulate well of feeling things he did not want to feel.

He kissed Jason with gentle insistence, parting his lips with his tongue, closing his eyes as though he was drinking in Jason's every response, every breath.

When he came it was with a long, long groan that seemed almost wrenched out of him, his hands closing on Jason's with bruising strength as his whole body spasmed, pouring out hot, sweet stickiness in what looked like an almost excruciatingly powerful orgasm.

Afterward they basked in the mellow lamplight, holding each other.

"What do you think about Montana?" Sam asked lazily. He picked up Jason's hand and kissed his palm almost absently before placing it on his own flat abdomen.

"It's big. It's got a lot of mountains. Why?"

"I like it."

"You mean…you like it enough to live here?"

Sam shrugged. "Who knows. You keep reminding me I'll have to retire one of these days." He smiled and traced the brown tan line across Jason's hips. "Of course, it's a long way from the ocean—and you're half fish."

Montana had some things going for it, fair enough. It was beautiful, no question. Maybe one of the most beautiful places Jason had ever been.

It wasn't just a matter of geography, though. Jason's career was on an upward trajectory, and some of that momentum inevitably had to do with location. The LA Field Office was one of the largest and most high-profile in the country. Los Angeles was arguably the current art capital of the nation. There were opportunities for him there that would not be available elsewhere. Certainly not in Siberia. Also, his parents were not young. Anywhere, Montana, was a long way from Los Angeles if he had to get home quickly.

"The winters would take some getting used to," Jason said.

"You would not enjoy the winters," Sam agreed.

Jason smiled. Not because the winters would probably kill him, but because of the casual way Sam threw out that *you*, as though taking it for granted that wherever he ended up, it would be with Jason.

They lay in contented silence for a while, Sam idly folding and smoothing out the fingers of Jason's hand resting on his abdomen.

"I met the president of your fan club today," Jason remarked. He glanced sideways at Sam.

"Hm?" Sam's brows shot up. "Oh." He was amused. "Petty. He's enthusiastic."

"Understatement."

"You're not jealous?" Sam sounded incredulous.

Jason thought it over. "I don't think so. No. You had a thing with him, I take it?"

Sam dipped his head left and right. *Comme ci, comme ça.* "'A thing' might be putting it too strongly. I like him. We had sex."

"Okay." He wanted to ask the obvious question, but pride kept him silent.

Sam seemed to reflect. "It was before I met you. Obviously."

Was it obvious? If so, Jason was glad to hear it.

He said, "Sure. Well, and even if it wasn't, we didn't have any agreement."

"No."

Jason chose his next words carefully. "It would bother me now."

Sam made a *hmph* sound. "I would hope."

Jason smiled, closed his eyes again. "Just wanted to be sure we're on the same page."

"There's nobody but you, West."

"I haven't wanted anyone else since we met."

Sam gave a funny laugh. "Except Chris Shipka."

Jason winced, looked up. "That was…" Something he preferred not to think about. He had been in a lot of pain and had made the mistake of thinking sex with someone—anyone—who wasn't Sam would help.

Into his silence, Sam said without inflection, "Yeah."

Jason said huskily, "I thought it was over between us."

*You said it was over.*

"I know." Sam added in afterthought, "I'm sorry."

Jason made a sound that didn't seem as much like a laugh as he'd hoped. "It was stupid."

"It's forgotten."

Well, no, it wasn't, since Sam had just brought it up again. They had never really talked about it until now. But then, what was there to say? They *both* knew why it had happened.

Jason said, "Petty is hoping a place in your BA unit might open up."

"Is he?" Sam sounded surprised and thoughtful. "That's… He might make a good choice."

"He's a little young, isn't he? Don't you need at least seven years as an active agent to be considered?"

"Usually. He's older than he looks. He's older than you, as a matter of fact. He's been an agent for six years. But, as with the ACT, sometimes exceptions are made."

"Older than *me*?"

Sam made a sound of amusement. "That's right, old man."

"Hm."

Maybe Jason *was* a little jealous because he did not like that idea. Any part of that idea, but particularly the part where Sam made exceptions for Travis Petty.

"Something to think about," Sam said. He yawned hugely, stretched, and turned out the lamp.

He was running.

Racing through a misty, wet woodland. The ground was sucking at his feet, dragging at him, and the harder he ran, the slower he seemed to be going. He was so *tired*. He had been running and running and running. He couldn't afford to slow down, couldn't stop, because *he* was right behind him, right *there*. He could hear him, feel him closing in—

Sam said calmly from close by, "You're dreaming, Jason."

Jason's eyes flew open. Another strange darkness. Another strange bed.

Another hotel room.

He had to catch his breath. His heart was still hammering. But he wasn't alone. That made a nice change.

"Right," he gulped. "Sorry." He was hell to sleep with these days.

Sam didn't answer, pulling him over, pressing Jason's damp head to his bare chest. Jason could hear the familiar rock-solid *thump* of Sam's heart beneath his ear.

He made himself lie still, taking long, careful breaths.

Sam was quiet too. He combed his fingers through Jason's hair, slow, untroubled passes over Jason's head like this was normal, like this was how everyone spent the night.

Jason's breathing quieted, his heart calmed.

He was glad Sam didn't ask him about the dream, didn't try to psychoanalyze him. It wasn't like there was any hidden meaning to be deciphered. Jason was in fear of his life. And with good reason.

Sam was still petting him, the pads of his fingertips circling Jason's scalp in small, soothing motions.

It was comforting, even sort of pleasurable, and little prickles rose on Jason's skin.

"Feels nice," he mumbled.

He was too tired to get worked up about it, but yeah. Nice.

Sam said, "My mother used to rub my head when I had trouble sleeping."

Jason huffed amusement. It was hard to imagine Sam ever lying still long enough for a head rub. It was hard imagining Sam as a little kid. But he'd seen the pictures to prove it.

"All those bees buzzing around your bonnet, no wonder you cain't sleep." Sam's droll mimicking of Ruby Kennedy's Western drawl won a tired laugh from Jason.

"Her secret weapon."

"One of them," Sam agreed.

He continued that slow, restful head massage, and Jason tried to convince himself he was going to drift off. Of course, the more he tried to tell himself he was sleepy, the less likely sleep was.

"It won't go on forever," Sam said after a time.

Jason moved his head in assent. Was that the good news or the bad news? Sometimes he wasn't sure.

"And I know you know this, but it's not just about situation awareness or staying sharp. You have to take care of yourself. Eat right. Sleep right." Sam added neutrally, "Go easy on the alcohol."

Jason grimaced. "I know."

Sam's fingertips lightly brushed his ribs. Jason amended, "I'm trying."

Sam didn't say anything else, or at least didn't verbalize anything else, but he was saying plenty through touch, and Jason let himself be reassured, comforted, by those silent caresses.

# CHAPTER SIX

*JOGGING* read the single word scribbled on Holiday Inn stationery.

Jason peered blearily at the paper on the pillow next to him, sighed, and dropped back to stare up at the ceiling sprinkler heads. Sam was by nature an early riser. Also a late-to-beder. In fact, he did not sleep much, period. Which was why waking him up in the middle of the night when he did finally manage to rest was really not okay.

But thank God he had been there last night. Last night… Last night Jason had needed a friend as well as a lover, and he was just very grateful Sam had been there.

But how the hell much longer was this going to go on?

Most of the time he was too busy to worry about— Well, that was a lie. He did not ever entirely forget that Kyser was out there. It was like knowing you had some dreaded virus sleeping in your bloodstream, something that hadn't manifested yet but was probably going to kill you one of these days.

Hopefully the Bureau would find the cure first, but there was no guarantee.

Jason heard the hotel room door slam as he was stepping out of the shower. He had delayed returning to his own room in hopes of a final few private moments with Sam. He already knew Sam was having breakfast with SAC Phillips, so that possibility was out.

He dried off—making sure to leave a clean towel for Sam—and opened the bathroom door.

Sam was on the phone, of course. He raised his brows in silent greeting.

"See you in twenty." He disconnected, tossed his phone to the bed. "Morning. Sleep okay?"

His face had a healthy flush beneath the sheen of perspiration. His hair was damp. He wore navy sweats and a sweat-stained navy T-shirt with the gold initials FBI.

"You mean the part of the night when I wasn't shouting down the house?"

"You don't talk in your sleep, let alone shout." Sam smiled faintly. "It's the only time you *don't* talk."

"*Hey.*"

But Jason was not offended. It was true. He was verbal. *Strong communication skills* was a notation on every report card and job evaluation he'd ever had. Not always a compliment.

He reached for his jeans, and Sam caught him by the arm and pulled him in for a kiss.

"Mm," Sam murmured regretfully. "I wish we had more time."

Jason smiled, not bothering to answer. Sam released him, and Jason pulled on his jeans and T-shirt.

"What have you got going on tonight?" He picked up his ankle holster and Glock. He had started wearing the ankle holster at Sam's insistence. Only on those occasions where he would not usually arm. He hated the damned thing with a passion and was convinced he was going to shoot himself in the foot one of these days, but if it made Sam happy…

Sam sighed. "Dinner with the SACs from four satellite offices."

Jason sighed too. "Okay. Will I see you later?"

"God, I hope so."

That was so heartfelt, Jason had to laugh. He was disappointed, but he had known there was a good chance the trip was going to go like this.

"Well, if you get away early, give me a call."

Sam's brows rose. "What's early?"

"Anything before seven a.m. tomorrow."

Sam snorted, pulled him in for a kiss.

After shaving, dressing in appropriate business attire in his own room, and arming, Jason texted J.J.

Lobby in 15, J.J. texted back.

Huh. Either things had gone very well the night before, or they had gone very wrong.

Jason had breakfast on his own—the Holiday Inn did a more than decent spread of pastries and DIY omelets if you were into eating—fueling up on coffee and answering the usual slew of emails that magically flooded his inbox at night.

He was tired, but not as tired as some mornings, and he was grateful to Sam for that. Mostly, his mind was on the upcoming meeting with Quilletta McCoy.

Having met Bert, the co-defendant in van Apeldoorn v. Thompson, he believed Quilletta was probably the driving force behind the efforts to dispose of Roy Thompson's estate. Not only had Bert directed them to speak to his big sister, Bert's taste in art seemed to run to comely Indian maidens and cowboys roping broncos. It seemed unlikely he'd recognize an Old Master if a Rembrandt in an ornate gilt frame fell on him.

Quilletta might not have known exactly what she had in Uncle Roy's treasure trove, but she had been smart enough to know she had something. She had sent the van Eyck to Christie's for appraisal, and after six months of researching provenance, Christie's had returned the painting.

Too hot to handle, in other words. Even for Christie's, which had gained a reputation for not always exercising due diligence when investigating the provenance of works with dubious histories.

Whatever Christie's had communicated to Quilletta, it had not discouraged her from trying to sell the work on the international art market—and two additional paintings as well.

He scrolled quickly through updates on active cases, frowned over news from Detective Gil Hickok, head of LAPD's Art Theft Detail, that Shepherd Durrand was rumored to be back in the States—possibly good news if it was true, or possibly not, if Shepherd knew something about his legal standing that they didn't. There were several new cases to consider: the theft of a Renoir from a residence on Catalina Island, yet another Internet art scam, and a complaint alleging a Beverly Hills vintage-wine merchant had committed fraud.

He was a little irritated—and would be first to admit, unreasonably—when he absently glanced up and spotted Travis Petty enter the lobby. Sam hadn't mentioned his morning ride to the office was Petty.

That would be because Sam didn't consider it worth mentioning, which was of course reassuring. Also further irritating.

Petty scanned the lobby, spotted Jason, hesitated—recognized that his hesitation was noticeable—and came over to Jason's table.

"West."

"Hey," Jason said with a cordiality he didn't feel. "Help yourself to coffee."

Petty's smile was off-hand. "No thanks. We're having breakfast in a couple of minutes."

*We?* Jason started to speak but caught himself. Maybe Petty was going to be at breakfast with Phillips and Sam. So what? Why not? The only legit cause he had for annoyance was at himself for having to struggle not to give in to irrational jealousy. He was not jealous by nature, so what the hell?

He said instead, "Sam should be down any second."

Petty nodded, glanced automatically at the elevators. When he turned back to Jason, his expression was odd. He said, "Did he tell you about me?"

Jason frowned. On the one hand, nice to know his instinctive unease regarding Petty was not misplaced. On the other, he had never been confronted with a situation like this, and he wasn't quite sure how to respond.

"Is there so much to tell?" he asked finally. Which probably wasn't tactful, but he didn't like this scenario. And he was quite sure Sam would like it even less.

Petty's smile was wry and unexpectedly appealing. "I thought there was. I guess not." He added thoughtfully, "This explains why he was different that last time."

Having been on the receiving end of Sam being "different," Jason could relate.

He opened his mouth—though he wasn't sure what he was going to say—but the elevator doors slid open, and Sam stepped out.

"Enjoy your breakfast." Jason raised a hand in brief greeting to Sam and then picked up his phone so he didn't have to watch them walk out together.

Even so, he couldn't help hearing that too eager note in Petty's voice as he told Sam good morning—and he couldn't help analyzing Sam's deep tones as he replied. Neutral? Guarded? Preoccupied?

The glass doors opened, the dry summer air wafted in, the doors closed.

J.J. appeared and went straight for the coffee urns.

Jason said, "We've got just enough time if you want breakfast. They've got your Cinnabons."

J.J. gave a full body shudder. "No. God no."

Jason stared at him. "Are you *hungover*?"

"A little." J.J. grimaced. He brightened momentarily. "That girl, West."

"Martinez?"

"She's a saint."

"That must cramp your style a little."

J.J. made a *ha-ha* face.

Jason was not unsympathetic, though. J.J. was still technically a new agent. He'd been in more gun battles his first year than most agents dealt with their entire careers. And now he had killed someone. Sure, they were trained for that possibility, but even so...

"We're supposed to meet de Haan at Quilletta McCoy's lawyer's office."

J.J. scowled. "De Haan's in on that meeting too?"

Jason nodded.

"Why are we allowing a civilian to take part in these interviews?"

"Because he's officially representing Aaldenberg van Apeldoorn. And because he's been working this case for nearly twenty years. We're working off his notes, his research. He knows a hell of a lot more about it than either of us do. About the case and about the treasure."

"Treasure." J.J. looked pained. "Can we not refer to it as treasure?"

"I don't know what else you'd call it," Jason said. "Fifteen missing items, including a platinum and diamond necklace, pearl and emerald earrings, two jeweled and enameled boxes, a gold locket, an altar piece by van Eyck, and nine very valuable—maybe even in one case priceless—paintings."

"It's the paintings *you* want," J.J. said. "Especially that Vermeer."

"If it is a Vermeer, yes, I'd like to be part of seeing that recovered. But it will go back to Amsterdam. It won't go to a museum here."

Or at least in principle that was what should happen. More often than not, museums, galleries, and even governments struggled with letting go national treasures—even another nation's treasures. Particularly items that had graced museum collections for decades. The ongoing battle for the Elgin Marbles was a perfect example.

Art and artifacts looted by the Nazis were especially problematic given that the documentation needed to prove provenance was often, understandably, missing. Even when it wasn't hard to prove legal ownership, museum curators had a way of fighting tooth and nail to keep valuable and popular exhibitions right where they were.

He sympathized a little. These were institutions dedicated to protecting and preserving art for the public. Most of the looted art was from private collections—the antithesis of a museum or gallery's mission.

In fairness, some of the reluctance to hand priceless antiquities back to their countries of origin had to do with unstable and dangerous political situations. The fate of museum collections and archeological sites in Egypt, Iraq, and Libya were all depressing cases in point.

It was almost certain that Roy Thompson's heirs were going to come up with some variation on that theme to explain their uncle's theft. Private collectors were always much, much worse about returning stolen items, and by now he had heard every excuse under the sun, including *I didn't think anyone would miss it.*

Seventy-something years later, over half of the hundreds of thousands of stolen pieces of art and objects recovered from the Nazis remained unaccounted for. Horrifyingly, much of those priceless works and personal treasures had gone missing during the allied occupation—much of it into personal collections.

"Whatever." J.J. tossed the rental car keys absently. "If you don't want media attention, you ought to stop saying the word *treasure*."

Good point.

Jason swallowed a final mouthful of coffee, dropped a couple of bills on the table, and followed J.J. out.

\* \* \* \* \*

Quilletta McCoy was not what Jason had expected.

True, he hadn't formed an opinion on what to expect, but it had not been this apologetic and red-cheeked church lady. Quilletta looked a little like a middle-aged, suburban Snow White. The early Disney version with the black bob and long-lashed doe eyes. She even had that same cute little squeaky voice.

The meeting, which took place in the cushy, leather-lined law offices of Corliss, Flook & Doggett, was attended by Quilletta, her brother, Bert—who looked like he was attending under pain of firing squad—and Dave Corliss, Quilletta's "lawyer and family friend."

"It was our understanding the statute of limitations had run out," Quilletta explained in tones as soft and sweet as confectioner's sugar. "That's what the man at Christie's told us."

"What man?" Jason questioned.

"That is a *lie*," de Haan broke in—which, of course, resulted in Corliss's protest.

"My client is making every effort to cooperate with the government and the Aaldenberg van Apeldoorn Museum. I'm not going to sit here and have her insulted."

"No insult is intended," Jason said, giving de Haan his most discouraging look. "We're simply gathering the facts of the case."

De Haan glowered but pressed his lips tightly closed.

Quilletta had turned even pinker at de Haan's outburst. She said to Jason, "I don't remember which man. We—" She glanced at her brother, who had not said a word beyond a gruff hello to Jason and J.J. "*I* spoke to several people at the auction house. They communicated that they would have liked to handle the altar piece and the paintings, but their organization had come under criticism for selling a painting that once belonged to Hermann Göring himself." Her dark eyes were wide with astonished memory.

"The Sisley," Jason agreed.

The 2018 sale of *Premier jour de printemps à Moret* to a Swiss art dealer was still a scandal in the art world. Christie's claimed every reasonable attempt had been made to check the painting's provenance, but with an entire department dedicated to researching looted art, it was a little hard to believe the ownership gaps in the Sisley's history hadn't raised red flags.

Nor was it the first time Christie's had been embroiled in a legal battle over looted art. So it was not impossible that someone at the auction house had communicated regret to Quilletta.

The part about the statute of limitations was harder to believe—Christie's was well informed on that topic. But maybe Quilletta had misunderstood something said to her.

"There isn't a universal statute of limitations regarding art stolen by the Nazis," Jason said. "The law is complicated, but under the 1998 Washington Conference, the US and the

Netherlands, along with about fifty other countries, committed to 'fair and just solutions' for the return of Nazi looted art. But that's beside the point because in 2016, the Ninth Circuit essentially ruled in a similar case that Dutch law applied, and Dutch law typically favors the claims of Dutch museums."

Corliss said, "That doesn't mean our lawsuit would have the same outcome."

"No. Not necessarily. But these items are not under any statute of limitations, which is my point."

"My uncle was not a thief," Quilletta said. Her voice wobbled, and tears filled her eyes. "He was given these items by his commanding officer so that they could be protected. It was a very dangerous situation. For the art as well as the soldiers."

Jason repeated, "He was *given* these items?"

"Yes."

Not good. Not good at all. Jason tensed, waiting for her to name that commanding officer. If she said Emerson Harley… It was not proof, but it certainly did not help Jason's case, given that in all of de Haan's copious research, *Emerson Harley*'s name was only referenced once, and that notation question-marked.

Jason had known the reference was correct because he knew his grandfather had, for a short time, been in charge of the recovery and restoration of the art stockpiled by the Nazis in the tunnels of Engelshofen Castle. It wasn't information readily available to someone trying to build a cover story after the fact.

Quilletta continued, "I remember Uncle Roy saying the paintings were being stored in damp and dirty conditions.

There was all kinds of thieving and pilfering going on. And the Russians were coming."

Jason glanced at de Haan.

They had expected to hear justification—that the art had been moved for its own safety—but until now Jason had assumed potential accusations against his grandfather would be of omission, negligence, or, worst case and the least likely scenario, willfully turning a blind eye to war-weary soldiers claiming war trophies. There was precedent. A few allied commanders had done that very thing despite Eisenhower's strict instructions that WWII would be different from all others in that no looting, no theft, no to-the-victors-go-the-spoils would be tolerated.

Quilletta's version of events was especially alarming because, if you didn't know Emerson Harley as Jason had, it might even sound plausible. A dedicated and desperate Monuments Man had violated his code of ethics and sworn duty because it was the only way to protect these priceless works.

Of course, on closer examination, such a claim made no sense because the whole point of Grandpa Harley being at Engelshofen Castle was to protect and preserve that discovered cache of art and oversee its return to its rightful owners. He had the knowledge and resources to accomplish his mission. Dispersing priceless works to troops with vague directives to ship them home and keep them safe would have been, at the least, counterproductive.

There were other problems with Quilletta's story. Some crazy and alarming things had happened in Bavaria after the war, that was true, but a Soviet invasion had not been one of them. The Russians had occupied *Eastern* Germany.

It sounded like maybe Quilletta was confusing her uncle's war stories with a viewing of the movie *The Monuments Men*. That didn't mean she was lying. She could inadvertently be quoting someone else's lies. Or she could just be confused. If there was one thing he had learned in this job, it was that people were very often confused in their facts—and just as often reluctant to admit it.

He said, "Mrs. McCoy, do you have *proof* your uncle was instructed to remove these items from where they were being guarded—"

"Proof be damned!" de Haan broke in. "No one had the right to disburse these paintings to anyone, nor bequeath them. What is of importance now is the itemization of the treasures in her possession."

Jason snapped, "We have to know what happened."

"We know enough! Assigning blame is secondary to our main concern."

"There is proof," Quilletta put in timidly.

De Haan was surprised into silence.

"By proof, do you mean you have written documentation?" Jason demanded.

She cast a nervous look at Corliss, who nodded. "I-I don't have it. It does exist. Or it used to. I did *see* it."

"Where did you see it? What documentation was there?"

He was trying to keep his tone noncommittal, but she must have heard something that further alarmed her. She licked her lips. "All the time he was overseas, Uncle Roy wrote letters home. I remember seeing them."

"Was the name or rank of this commanding officer mentioned?"

"Yes. I think so. I believe so. I don't remember what it was. It's been years since I saw the letters."

De Haan opened his mouth. Jason said quickly, "What happened to the letters?"

He could feel both de Haan and J.J. staring at him. Or maybe that was just his guilty conscience. His question was valid. Maybe not priority in the ordinary way of things. Priority for him.

"I-I don't remember."

Bert said suddenly, "Doc has them, doesn't he?"

"Does he?" Quilletta looked blank.

"Who's Doc?" Jason asked.

"Doc Roberts. Edgar Roberts," Bert said. "He and Uncle Roy were...friends."

What did...*friends* mean?

"I see. So, to your best knowledge, this Edgar Roberts has possession of the letters which you say prove your uncle was ordered by a commanding officer to take these items and ship them back home?"

"Yes. Well, I mean, I don't know," Quilletta said. "I know the letters prove Uncle Roy was not a thief. It was never *his* idea to move those items. Never. He would have as easily thought of moving the moon. But I don't know for a fact that Edgar has them. I don't know why he would. If it matters, all Uncle Roy's letters home were published in the *Bozwin Daily Chronicle*."

Jason's heart stopped. He could think of absolutely nothing to say.

*Published.*

A weird silence seemed to fall over the office.

Jason felt J.J.'s glance, but could honestly not find the words he needed. This was a disaster he had not counted on.

J.J. said, "Regarding the items not already listed for sale—"

Quilletta said quickly, "But that's just it. That's why Bert and I wanted this meeting. We don't want trouble. We don't have money for a big lawsuit. We don't want the IRS to come after us. We're willing to work with the government and the museum and the-the heirs of the other two paintings, if there are any still living, but we don't have those other things." She nodded at de Haan. "The things listed in the email he sent. We don't have them. We never did."

# Chapter Seven

"She's lying," de Haan said.

De Haan, J.J., and Jason were sitting in a downtown restaurant and bakery called the Coffee Pot, holding an impromptu council of war after leaving the meeting at Corliss, Flook & Doggett.

"I don't know," J.J. said through a mouthful of freshly baked cinnamon roll. "If she's lying, she's pretty convincing."

De Haan scoffed at the idea.

"If they *don't* have the other items, where are they?" J.J. asked thoughtfully. "Who has them?"

Jason listened absently. His thoughts were running in circles. He needed to go through the newspaper morgue at the *Bozwin Daily Chronicle* and find out what, if anything, Captain Thompson had written about Emerson Harley. It was possible the archive was already digitized and online—thanks to Google's aborted News Archive Project, thousands of newspapers and millions of pages had been scanned and made available to anyone with time and patience to sort through them all. But physical newspaper archives sometimes contained supplemental materials. Things like photos, internal correspondence, reporters' notes, or perhaps the original letters from a homesick GI Joe. It was worth checking.

It was unlikely Thompson's family would have handed over any letters for publication that mentioned sending art treasures home. Almost certainly Thompson would have warned them to keep quiet about the parcels he was shipping under separate cover. It was equally unlikely that a newspaper of the day would have published anything derogatory about the military or military officers. But Thompson could have easily mentioned his commanding officers in an innocuous context.

That was the kind of information a good reporter would hunt down. After that, it wouldn't be difficult to connect the dots.

And not everyone cared if the dots created a completely false picture. Sometimes members of the press just wanted a good story—and damn the personal cost to the subjects of that false narrative.

There wouldn't be just one commander in Captain Thompson's life. Emerson Harley's mission had been tangential to that of the 3rd Infantry Division. Thompson would have had to answer to a whole chain of command. But this was a story about stolen art, so even if Thompson did not specifically point the finger at Harley, the Deputy Chief of the Monuments, Fine Arts, and Archives program was naturally going to be the prime suspect.

And if Quilletta was right, if her uncle did name Harley in his letters, it was going to be case closed in the eyes of a lot of people.

Which was one more reason why Jason had been reluctant to hand this case over to anyone else. Generally speaking, the ACT liked—and typically received—good press. Another agent was not going to do his best to make sure the story of Thompson's treasures was DOA. Just the opposite.

"All fifteen items disappeared at the same time," de Haan said. "It's too great a coincidence that two thieves should be at work."

"Maybe they were working together," J.J. said.

De Haan scoffed at this idea, and J.J. glanced at Jason.

"West?"

Jason snapped out of his preoccupation. "Hm?"

"Something bugging you?"

"No. Just thinking." He hit rewind on the last few seconds of conversation. "It's possible Thompson had a partner. It's also possible—"

"Yes, this Emerson Harley, the officer who gave him permission to take the works from the castle. We know he was complicit in the theft," de Haan said.

So much for hoping de Haan might have forgotten the name of that mysterious officer. It was like discovering you had stepped on a landmine—again. Everything in Jason froze... and then defrosted in a wave of anger. But that was irrational. De Haan wasn't the bad guy. He was simply drawing logical conclusions from the information available to them. He was thinking like a good investigator.

"We don't know that," Jason said. "We don't know there was any such officer."

"I agree," J.J. said. "That sounds like a bullshit excuse to me."

"What are you saying? We have the man's name," de Haan objected. "*Emerson Harley*. The McCoy woman says there is proof."

Every time he heard his grandfather's name, Jason flinched internally. He tried to clarify without actually stepping into the zone of possible obstruction. "Harley existed, yes, but there would have been other officers around too. We don't yet have proof that *any* of them were involved with Thompson."

"It's Thompson's word against whatever this Harley will say," J.J. agreed.

"Harley is dead," de Haan said dismissively. "Perhaps you are right. But I believe Quilletta is lying. She is hiding something."

For an instant Jason was paralyzed by the realization that de Haan had done preliminary research on his grandfather—and could easily have stumbled across Jason's personal connection.

He missed the next bits of conversation, before managing to say, "She might not be lying. She might not have all the facts to begin with. I think she's legitimately afraid of further lawsuits."

Bert's...*friend* comment popped into his mind. Bert's expression had been...what?

He added, "Bert Thompson, however, is hiding something, that's for sure."

And not just the obvious something. Something more. Something Quilletta didn't know?

"Bert?" J.J. sounded surprised.

Jason nodded.

"I didn't get that. He didn't say more than ten words the whole time."

"We must get a search warrant," de Haan said. "We must search Thompson's house for the missing treasure."

"Thompson's house is Quilletta's home now," J.J. said. "She got the house. Bert got the flower shop."

That was one of the things that worried Jason. Roy Thompson had not been a rich man, but he'd been comfortably off. In addition to real estate and a small but lucrative business, he'd been able to leave his niece and nephew each a hundred thousand dollars. Was that financial cushion the result of quietly selling off stolen art treasures over the years?

De Haan thought not. De Haan had been tracking these individual pieces for decades, waiting for them to show up on the international art market, and he believed the treasure was still intact. But then, he *wanted* to believe it was intact. They all did.

"Anyway, we'd have to have a hell of a lot more evidence than we currently do to get a search warrant," J.J. said. "No judge is going to grant one based on what we've got so far."

De Haan turned to Jason.

"Agent Russell is right," Jason said. "The Thompsons are ostensibly cooperating with us. We don't have any proof they possess the missing items. If they do have them, why wouldn't they have put them up for sale at the same time as the altar piece and the two paintings?"

"They may have been testing the waters."

"Maybe. Or they're telling the truth. They don't have the rest of the treasure."

"Then the accomplice has them," J.J. said. "We need to figure out who *that* guy was."

Jason said, "Okay, again, we don't know that there was an accomplice. And even if there was, we don't know if it was a fellow soldier—"

"But it was," de Haan insisted. "It was the officer Harley. We must find out more about this mystery man. If we speak to his family..."

"Emerson Harley," J.J. mused. "Why does that name sound familiar?"

"*No!*" Jason burst out.

De Haan and J.J. gaped at him. Jason controlled himself with an effort.

"What I mean is, yes, of course, we have to follow up on *that*, but we can't afford to make assumptions. It's very unlikely Thompson's commanding officer, let alone a member of the MFAA, gave any such order. If you understand anything about the Monuments Men, you'll see it's...it's ludicrous."

"Most of the thefts were by officers," de Haan pointed out. "Officers had access to places enlisted men could not go. They could move items without being questioned."

That, unfortunately, was true.

"Not the MFAA," Jason said. "These weren't regular soldiers. They were art historians, museum curators, archivists, teachers, artists. A lot of them were too old to be drafted, so they enlisted. They voluntarily chose to go into battle zones, to risk their lives so that they could protect the art treasures of the world. And they stayed on after the war to oversee the return of something like five million cultural objects. There were Monuments Men in Europe all the way to 1951."

De Haan shrugged. J.J. was still studying Jason. "What's your theory?"

"I don't have a theory yet. I just— We have to remember that if Thompson had an accomplice, it wasn't necessarily someone in his squad. Or regiment. Or even division. And it needn't have been a friend. Or maybe it was a friend but in another division. It could have been someone in, I don't know… The shipping depot. When he started mailing all these parcels home, why did no one question it? *Or*, it could have been a Bavarian national."

"A girl," de Haan said. "Perhaps there was a romance—"

"Nah," J.J. said. "I think Thompson was gay."

Momentarily distracted, it was Jason's turn to stare.

J.J. shrugged, explained to de Haan, "I always get partnered with gay agents. I have a sixth sense about this."

Jason's mouth dropped open.

"No, but seriously," J.J. said.

*"Seriously?"*

"Yes. Seriously. I knew you were gay the minute I met you."

"Wouldn't that be a sexth sense?" Jason retorted, resisting the impulse to conk J.J. with the metal napkin holder.

De Haan just looked confused. He smiled uncertainly at Jason, who shook his head.

J.J. continued blithely on with his theory. "So yeah, I think maybe there was a boy in Bavaria."

*The Boy from Bavaria.* It sounded like a schlocky spy movie from the 1970s.

"Anyway," Jason said, "mystery accomplices aside, the other problem we've got is the Thompsons have lived here forever. They have roots in the community; they're respected business owners and neighbors. We're the feds, and you're working for a foreign country. That's how a local judge is liable to look at this if we can't supply a hell of a lot more probable cause for a search warrant."

"What are you saying?" de Haan demanded. "The fight is over?"

Jason said, "No. Of course not. We're moving forward on recovering the items they put up for sale. And we're going to continue to investigate what happened to the items still unaccounted for. If it looks like we have grounds, we'll get a search warrant."

"I will tell you what will happen to those items. The Thompsons will sell them quietly, secretly, through other channels."

J.J. looked at Jason.

"I don't think so," Jason said. "Not immediately. They think—and rightly—that we're watching them. If they do have the items and believe they're successfully hiding them from us—and that's a huge supposition right there—they'll wait, let the heat die down before they try anything else."

De Haan was not happy with this. "I don't think the Thompsons are as clever as you are, Jason. I think they are prone to act quickly and foolishly."

"Maybe, but for now our hands are tied," Jason said.

And with that de Haan had to be content. Or discontented. J.J. finished his late breakfast, they promised de Haan they would be in touch, and Jason and J.J. left the restaurant.

"Something wrong?" J.J. asked as they were driving back to the office.

Jason glanced at him. "No."

"Because you seem off."

"*I* do?"

J.J. glanced around as though looking for someone in the back seat. He turned to Jason. "Yes. *You* do. You've been tense and short-tempered ever since we left the lawyer's office. I thought you were going to take poor Hans Brinker's head off a couple of times at breakfast."

Jason tried to summon a smile. "No. Just…short of sleep."

"It's the Vermeer, right?" J.J. was sardonic. "You had your heart set on restoring a lost Vermeer to the world."

"That would have been nice," Jason agreed.

"Well, maybe it's still out there somewhere."

"Maybe."

J.J. gave him another of those sideways looks. "Should I book our flights back to LA?"

"LA?" Jason said blankly.

J.J. made a sound of disbelief. "You remember LA, West. Tall buildings, smog, traffic, our homes and family and friends. *Our jobs.*"

"Right. LA," Jason said. "Um, I think we should hold off for a day or so. We still have people to interview, including Edgar Roberts. If he's of an age with Thompson, maybe they were overseas at the same time. We have to interview Thompson's great-niece—now there's something. Thompson had two great-nieces, but only one was mentioned in his will."

"Bad blood between Bert and his uncle?"

"Maybe. But Bert's in the will."

J.J. shrugged. "Okay. Something to follow up, I guess."

"And we have to interview his friends and neighbors and employees to find out what, if anything, they saw or heard about his treasures."

"Seriously. Please stop calling them treasures. I feel like one of the Hardy Boys."

Jason gave a reluctant laugh. "Also, I want to check the newspaper morgue. See what information we can get on possible accomplices."

"This mysterious commanding officer of Thompson's."

"Right."

"Those archives have to be digitized," J.J. said. "We shouldn't have to go through everything here."

"Are you in a hurry to get back?" Jason asked.

"Hell no. But if you're delaying on my account…"

That was almost funny. "Of course not."

Seemingly unconvinced, J.J. glanced away from the road to scrutinize him. "You *do* think that Vermeer is here," he said slowly, shrewdly.

Much, *much* better that J.J. focused on that angle than giving serious consideration to other possibilities.

"It's not impossible. But either way, there are still plenty of avenues to explore. Thompson may have insured the items, he may have tried to have them appraised, he may have attempted to research their background. All those efforts would leave footprints."

"And he may have known better than to do any of that."

"Yes. But what we do know for sure is he was a collector, and one thing all collectors have in common is a desire to show off their collections. If Thompson did bring back other treasures, there's a good chance he showed them to *some*one."

Back in the office, J.J. headed straight for Martinez's cubicle, and Jason headed straight for the restroom to splash some cold water on his face.

A glance at his dripping reflection in the mirror over the bank of sinks was not reassuring. Hopefully, some of it was the greenish fluorescent lighting, but he looked very tired and very pale. His eyes were fever-bright in his drawn face. No surprise J.J. was wondering what was up with him.

He bent over the sink, splashed on more water, and the door to the restroom swung open and Sam strolled in.

"Hey, how goes it?" Jason said.

Proof of Sam's preoccupation, he only then seemed to notice who the restroom's other occupant was. "Fine. You?"

Jason grabbed a paper towel and mopped his face. "Fine."

There must have been something in his voice because Sam said, "You okay?"

"Yep!"

Sam's eyes narrowed. "You sure?"

"Yeah, of course." There was nothing like people thinking you were acting oddly to make you start acting oddly. Jason winked. "Maybe a little sleep deprived."

Sam nodded thoughtfully. "Okay. Well, I'll talk to you this evening."

"Yes. Looking forward to it." Jason delivered a smile so brilliant, he nearly broke his face, and exited the bathroom.

J.J. had that cat-who-ate-the-canary look when Jason strode into their office.

He started to speak, but Jason cut him off. "Hey, I've been thinking. Why don't we split up this afternoon? That way we can cover more ground quickly."

J.J.'s smug smile faded. He gave an irritated sigh. "I knew it. I'm getting stuck going through the newspaper archives."

"No. Not at all," Jason said. "I'll take the archives."

J.J. rolled his eyes. "Oh. Right. Because you don't trust me to go through the archives on my own."

Would this be funny one day? Because right now…not.

Jason said with strained patience, "If you *want* to tackle the morgue—"

"Of course I don't."

"Exactly. So I'll take the archives, and you can start laying the groundwork for getting that search warrant."

"Which I'm going to do how?"

"Why don't you start by hunting down everyone who worked with or for Thompson? I think it would help if we had a better picture of who this guy was. It would give us insight into whether he was someone who might have taken an accomplice or been chosen as someone else's accomplice. It might tell us whether it was more likely he was working alone."

J.J. nodded thoughtfully. "Before the war, he taught art at a local college. After the war, he opened a florist shop. Why the career change?"

"Right. Exactly," Jason said. "We should find out more about his family. And of course, the main thing we want to know is did he ever talk about his collection with his employees, friends, lovers, enemies, neighbors, mailman..."

"Why would he?"

"Because that's what collectors do."

"If you say so."

"I do say so. So, can you handle that?"

J.J. said, "I can handle that, West. Keep your hair on."

"Great. Let's synchronize our watches—" He snorted at J.J.'s expression. "Kidding. But keep me posted, okay?"

"Where are you going? The newspaper?"

"Eventually, yeah. Maybe I'll have a word with Edgar Roberts first."

J.J. frowned. "You don't want to interview him together?"

"Covering more ground, right?" Jason reminded him.

He shrugged. "Your call."

"Keep me posted."

"You said that."

Jason let the door to the office swing shut behind him.

# CHAPTER EIGHT

Edgar "Doc" Roberts was trimming the wall of yellow roses surrounding his picture-perfect front yard when Jason parked before the gray and white 1920s bungalow, just a block away from busy Main Street in downtown Bozwin.

Roberts was a tall, slightly stooped elderly man in baggy denims and a faded turquoise Hawaiian shirt. He wore a wide-brimmed straw hat and lime-green flip-flops, and carried a deadly looking pair of gardening shears. As Jason got out of the car, Doc pulled his hat off, wiped his face on his arm, and replaced the hat.

"Howdy," he called as Jason strode up the flagstone walk.

"Hi." Jason flashed his badge. "Special Agent West, FBI. May I have a word, sir?"

"I figured you were some kind of cop." Doc took the proffered leather wallet. "FBI. Well, isn't that something?" He took his time examining Jason's ID and badge. "Looks just like it does in the movies," he marveled.

Jason smothered a grin. He suspected Doc was pulling his leg a little, but he had a soft spot for old-timers like Doc. They reminded him of his grandfather.

Finally, Doc handed back the wallet. "I've been expecting you. Well, someone like you. Why don't we go inside where it's cooler?"

Jason followed Doc up the stone walk to the wide wooden porch, and they went inside. It *was* cooler inside, and the house smelled agreeably of lemon furniture polish and linseed oil.

The interior was as pristine as the front yard, also unexpectedly and charmingly updated with distressed hardwood floors, brick-colored accent walls, and faux brick panels. A geometrically precise arrangement of framed black and white photos adorned the entryway. Jason examined several shots of a grinning younger version of Doc.

"You were with the 101st Airborne?"

Doc looked surprised. "You know your military insignia. That's right. The Screaming Eagles."

Doc had been a paratrooper. He had not been with the 3rd Infantry Division when they took Engelshofen Castle. So that was one obvious possibility eliminated.

Jason considered a couple of wooden-framed oil paintings on the wall. Europe. Maybe Germany. Maybe Bavaria. Maybe not. They were nice, though. Not Old Masters nice, but pleasing to the eye and better than the usual amateur effort.

"Are these your work?" Jason asked.

Doc laughed delightedly. "Now how did you know that?"

"I'm FBI. We know everything," Jason deadpanned.

Doc guffawed. "That's a good one. What would you like to drink, Agent West? I've pretty much got everything. Would you like to try a Montana margarita?"

"Water would be great," Jason said. "Ice tea if you have it."

Doc stopped beaming. "Now, I meant a real drink. I have to tell you: I don't trust a man who doesn't like to drink."

"I wouldn't trust a man who drinks on the job," Jason retorted.

Doc burst out laughing again. He beckoned Jason into the kitchen, where he set about throwing ice and tequila and margarita mix into a blender.

"I know why you're here, of course. Quilletta has started selling Roy's pictures, hasn't she?"

Jason opened his mouth to answer, but Doc turned on the blender.

When the blender stopped, Doc said, "Don't believe a word she says. That little gal lies like a rug. But you know, there's not a mean bone in her body. And the things she's had to contend with. Imagine: *two* husbands running off on her. The first bastard leaving her with a baby girl and a mountain of debt."

Once again, Jason tried to speak, and once again Doc turned on the blender.

When the whirring stopped, Doc said, "Bert's a different story. He's a born and bred asshole."

"I didn't realize that took a lot of breeding."

"More than you might think, Agent West. Homophobia is alive and well in the wild, wild West. I'll give him credit, he's been a good father to Patty and a good husband to Cindy. He wasn't much of a nephew, though."

Another burst of whirring ice.

Jason tried to hang on to his patience. That Spanish saying about the rich and the mighty? The elderly did not like to be rushed either.

The blender stopped, and Doc poured the frosty pale-green contents into two margarita glasses the size of small parachutes. He brought one to Jason, who took it with a sigh.

"Geronimo," Doc said, holding out his glass.

Jason clinked rims and put his glass down.

"Hey, that's bad luck," Doc protested.

"Sir—"

"Call me Doc. Everyone does." Doc slurped his margarita, licked his lips. "You don't know what you're missing, Agent West."

"Doc, what can you tell me about Roy Thompson?"

"What did you want to know?"

"Anything would be helpful at this point. He's a little bit of an enigma. What was he like? What kind of man was he?"

"I guess he was an ordinary guy. He had his strengths, and he had his weaknesses. Like the rest of us. He was loyal to his friends. He was generous to a fault. He was proud and didn't forgive insults easily. And he was easily insulted. He was a good son and a good brother and a good uncle. He wasn't a churchgoer. He wasn't a hypocrite." Doc shrugged like there was nothing else to say.

"When did you meet?"

Doc shook his head, picked up Jason's untouched glass, and quaffed the margarita in two gulps.

"Roy and I met at Gallatin County High School. In Mrs. Kaynor's tenth grade art class. And we stayed friends till the day Roy died. I guess we're still friends."

"Were you ever more than friends?"

"There's nothing more than friends, Agent West. Friends are the most important relationships we have. They're the family we pick."

"Sure," Jason said. "Were you ever romantically involved with Roy?"

Doc considered. "I don't know if it was ever what I'd call *romance*. After the war, we used to keep each other company sometimes."

"You were with the 101st where during the war?"

Doc said drolly, "Well, there was this little place called Normandy. You may have heard of it."

Jason nodded, conceding a point. "Sure. And thank you for your service, sir. Were you ever in Bavaria?"

Doc laughed heartily at the idea, but Jason was pretty sure the Screaming Eagles *had* been in Bavaria. Maybe not in May 1945, but at some point. He'd spent *a lot* of time listening to his grandfather talk about the war.

"You and Roy didn't serve together?"

"No. Different units entirely."

Being in Bavaria was a link, but not enough of a link. Still, not necessarily a complete dead end.

"You and Roy shared an interest in art. Was Roy a painter too?"

"He wanted to be." Doc said regretfully, "He just wasn't very good."

"But he taught art for a while. He collected art."

"Sure."

"Did Roy show you his art collection?"

"Sure. Roy showed everyone his collection."

If that was true, that would sure make his and J.J.'s job easier.

"Can you describe what you remember of his collection?"

Doc said vaguely, "His taste was eclectic. There were some things he bought from local dealers, things he picked up at art shows, things he bought on eBay, though I used to warn him not to trust those descriptions."

"And some things he shipped back from Europe during the war," Jason said.

"Now that I couldn't say."

"That's what his family says."

"Like I told you, Agent West, I wouldn't take anything Quilletta tells you too seriously."

"What about you? Did you bring back a few souvenirs?"

Doc said dryly, "We all brought back souvenirs of one kind or another."

"Did you bring back art?"

"No." He was definite on that point.

"The Thompson family tried to sell a panel from a van Eyck altar piece," Jason said. "That, along with a couple of valuable paintings they also put up for auction, was part of a trove of art looted by the Nazis and stored in Bavaria."

"Well, I'll be damned," Doc said wonderingly. "Looks like some of Roy's eBay buys paid off after all."

Jason was both amused and exasperated. "Doc—"

Doc glanced at the clock above the refrigerator. "I don't want to be inhospitable, but I've got to get to a doctor's appointment in a little bit. Once you get to be my age, doctor appointments are the highlight of your social calendar. Was there any-thing else you wanted to know?"

"Yes. There are plenty of other things I want to know. Did Roy ever mention the name Emerson Harley to you?"

Doc squinted as though watching a distant parade fade from sight. "I don't think so."

Was he telling the truth? He sounded sincere. Jason relaxed a little. "What about his letters? I understand you have those in your possession."

Doc raised his brows. "Whose letters?"

"Roy's."

"His *letters*? What kind of letters?"

"Letters he wrote during the war."

"We didn't write each other during the war. You wouldn't want to put anything on paper you wouldn't say to a room full of people. The censors were watching everything."

"Not to y—" Jason caught the glint in Doc's eyes and realized he was being led down another rabbit hole. "He wrote letters to his family, some of which were published in your local paper."

Doc said reminiscently, "That used to happen back then. People were eager to hear from the boys overseas. A lot of papers used to print letters like that. Roy had a colorful turn of phrase."

"Right. But do you know what happened to the original letters? To Roy's letters that weren't published in the paper."

"I guess the family would have those."

"Bert says he believes you have his uncle's letters."

"Bert wouldn't know his ass from a hole in the ground."

Jason smiled. "You didn't answer the question, Doc."

Doc tipped his head, regarding Jason. "I'll tell you what, Agent West. You come back and have a real drink with me some evening, and maybe I'll tell you what you want to know." He grinned. "Or maybe I won't."

**S**o okay.

It could have gone better, but then it could have gone worse too.

Doc almost certainly had those letters of Roy's. Whether he would hand them over remained to be seen. It wasn't unusual to have to interview witnesses more than once in complicated cases, and this case was nothing if not complicated.

As Jason walked down the peaceful shady street to his rental car, he tried to decide how much of what Doc had told him was the truth. On the whole, he thought Doc had been candid. He had tried to avoid outright lies. But he had also prevaricated. He might not know everything, but he knew more than he had been willing to share.

He had not seemed to recognize the name Emerson Harley. That was a relief. Not conclusive, of course, but moving in the right direction.

He would take Doc up on his offer and come back another time. Sometimes it took a while to establish trust.

Unfortunately, *a while* was a luxury Jason did not have.

# CHAPTER NINE

Jason had just turned the key in the ignition when he noticed a familiar blue compact rental car pull up across the street from Doc's house.

De Haan got out of the car and crossed the street.

Jason turned off the car engine and went to intercept him.

De Haan spotted him, checked, and his narrow face took on a defiant look.

"What are you doing here, Hans?" Jason asked.

De Haan straightened his shoulders, as if bracing for the reprimand he knew was coming. "The same thing as you, I think."

"The difference being I'm an agent of the federal government and you're—"

De Haan burst out, "I'm not breaking any laws. I have a right to ask questions."

"And these people have a right not to answer them. Look, it's not about: *do you have a right*; it's about what's going to get the results we need. If you start duplicating my efforts, that's liable to end with our witnesses shutting down and refusing to talk to either of us. They're not eager to talk now."

"I can't sit and do nothing."

"You can if it's the best way to get results." Jason hardened his heart. "Maybe it's time to go home."

"Go home!" De Haan looked aghast.

"Yes. You've done what you can do. You've got to let us take it from here."

"I can't do that. I will not do that."

"Hans…" Jason struggled for restraint. He threw a quick look back at Doc's house, and lowered his voice. "You came to me because you thought I could bring about your desired outcome to all your years of investigation, which is the return of these stolen artworks. Isn't that true?"

"Yes. But you've not been able to do this. At every turn they lie and deny. Our progress has stalled."

"For God's sake. I've just *started*. You've got to give me a little time. We've already managed to get Quilletta and Bert to agree to come back to the negotiating table for the van Eyck and the two paintings currently up for auction."

"They have no choice. There is an injunction to stop the sale."

"But they're not appealing. That's good. That's what we want. They're showing a willingness to cooperate with the museum."

"They deny having the other items. They deny the Vermeer."

"Yes. They do. Which is why I need to continue my investigation. I'm not taking them at their word. But I also don't have proof that they're lying." Jason added, "And as far as the Vermeer goes, we don't know that the painting described on the inventory list *was* a Vermeer."

"It is the exact description."

"It's very similar, I know, but—"

"I can *feel* it's here." De Haan put his hand over his heart. "I *know* they have it."

Jason was abruptly reminded of J.J. and his "sixth sense" about gay people. He sighed. "Okay, but that's not proof."

"Let me get the proof!"

"That's my job. Not yours."

"But I am not bound by the same rules and regul—"

"*Stop*," Jason snapped.

De Haan stopped, looking startled and then a little wounded.

Jason said more evenly, "Stop and listen to me. We want the *same* thing."

And that was true. Yes, Jason wanted additional things—proof that his grandfather was not involved in the theft—but the end goal was the restoration of these valuable treasures to their homeland. If somehow, unbelievably, his grandfather *had* been involved in the removal of these works of art, it was all the more important to Jason that he be the one to deliver them back to their rightful places. It was on him to make reparation, restitution.

"Hans, I'm on your side," Jason said. "If you 'know' anything, you know that."

De Haan met Jason's gaze. His shoulders slumped. "Yes."

"I know it's not easy, but trust me a little longer. I promise I'll keep you updated every step of the way, but you've got to let me do my job."

De Haan wavered, clearly torn. "You'll phone me this evening with everything you've learned?"

"Whether I've learned anything or not, I'll call you and bring you up to speed."

De Haan shook his head as though he did not believe it, but finally he turned away.

Jason watched until de Haan got into his car and drove off before returning to his own vehicle.

\* \* \* \* \*

He was pushing through the glass front doors of the Bozwin satellite office when someone jumped out of the hedge and snapped his photo.

For a moment Jason was so enraged, he considered tackling the guy and beating him with his own camera. And it must have shown on his face because the reporter stepped back, spreading his arms like *all's fair in love and news, right?*

And yeah, that was right, but Jason still wanted to kill him, not least because for one shocked instant, he had thought something very different was happening. He had not been ready for it, which scared him a little.

He had to stay ready. Kyser could come at him again at any time.

No harm, no foul. This had not been Kyser, this had not been that moment, but whether today's photo op had to do with yesterday's shooting or with word leaking out about why he and Russell were in town, having his picture in the paper was a bad idea.

*Shit.*

He continued into the office, made his way through the mini maze of cubicles and desks and offices. It was funny how every satellite office looked basically the same. Potted plants on desks, bulletin boards with calendars showing days checked off to the next vacation, framed family photos. By now even the people in the family photos were starting to look familiar.

As he passed the conference room, he glimpsed Sam leaning back in his chair, arms folded, watching approvingly as Agent Petty drew what appeared to be astrological symbols on a whiteboard.

It did not improve his mood any.

"Good, you're back," J.J. greeted him when he walked into their office. "How'd it go?"

"I'm going to have to talk to him again. De Haan arrived as I was leaving."

"*De Haan?* What the hell with that guy? You're going to have to do something about him."

"What do you suggest?"

"I don't know. You're supposed to be the diplomatic one. And if diplomacy fails, shoo—"

J.J. cut off mid-word. They stared at each other. J.J. picked up a notepad. "Here's what I've got so far on our principals. Quilletta, get this, is a former Miss Montana. That's her second claim to fame. She's never had any trouble with the law. She's an administrative assistant—a well-paid administrative assistant—at the Big Sky Federal Credit Union."

Jason nodded, only half listening. He was still rattled by the incident outside the building. He hadn't even noticed the man lurking in the hedge. How could he not have noticed? He *had* to be more vigilant.

"Her first husband ran off with his high-school sweetheart. They live in Arizona now. I've got a call in to him. Her second husband ran off with some bimbo he met online. I guess it wasn't just online, because he got her pregnant, from what I hear. Anyway."

Jason looked up. "What about Bert?"

"Clean slate there too. He married late in life. His wife's a lot younger. Same age as his niece, as a matter of fact. She was pregnant when they met. That baby grew up to be Patty, the girl Brody Stevens was trying to kill, I guess, when he shot up the Big Sky Guest Ranch."

Jason didn't miss that *trying to kill, I guess*. That was the awful truth. Brody Stevens might not have meant to kill Patty or anyone else. He might have just been trying to get her attention. That was the trouble when you mixed guns and bozos.

"What's Bert's credit report say?"

"He's a better cowboy than he is a businessman. Even with the money he inherited from his uncle, they're underwater financially. Everything's mortgaged to the hilt."

"Interesting. Okay. He needs the money the sale of the art would bring."

"Urgently."

"What about the niece? The great-niece, I mean. Quilletta's daughter."

J.J. consulted his notes. "Oh. Right. Terry "Baby" Mayhew. Thirty-nine, married, a stay-at-home…housewife, I guess. She doesn't work. No kids. Her husband, Gary, is forty and owns what appears to be a profitable garage here in town. But here's something interesting. Gary has a record."

Jason looked up. "He does?"

"Yep. B&E with a side of burglary. He did time. He was twenty-one."

"Twenty-one?" Jason weighed and discarded. "He hasn't been in trouble since?"

"He hasn't been *caught* since."

"Point. And it demonstrates a willingness to break laws." He thought back. "You said Quilletta had two claims to fame."

J.J. chuckled. "She and Ronnie McCoy, husband #2, were king and queen three years running of the Annual Winter Squash Festival."

Jason snorted. "And you tell me he ran off and left it all behind?"

"Sadly, it seems he gave up the squash for a squeeze."

Jason laughed, shook his head.

J.J. eyed him, hesitated, said, "Has Phillips spoken to you?"

"No. Why?"

"She told me Duane Jones is going to be arraigned on attempted homicide charges."

For a second, Jason could not remember who Duane Jones was. Oh. Right. The kid who had been driving the truck. The survivor.

No, *one* of the survivors.

"Sounds about right to me."

"Yeah." J.J. asked, "Do you think we should have heard something by now?"

"About what?"

"About yesterday? From the SIRG, I mean."

"No, it's too way soon. They'll still be interviewing witnesses and going over the forensics. We probably won't know for another month."

J.J. nodded, only half-listening.

Jason said, "If there was any question as to whether we acted appropriately, we would not be sitting here on the job right now."

"Yeah, I know."

Jason continued to survey his partner. "Everything okay?"

J.J. shrugged. "I guess. I'm waiting for the other shoe to drop."

"I don't think there are more shoes. I think this was a one-legged bandit."

J.J. smiled politely, absently.

"Have you spoken to George?" Jason asked.

"Of course."

Jason hesitated. "You know, if you do need to talk to someone—"

J.J. burst out laughing. "*You're* offering to counsel me?"

"Hell no." Jason was equally staggered at the idea. "I'm just saying there are resources available to you. I had counseling after Miami. There isn't any shame in it. It helped."

"You were shot in Miami. That's a little different."

"Yes. It was a different traumatic event. The point is—"

"This wasn't traumatic," J.J. interrupted. "Brody Stevens stalked and harassed his ex-girlfriend—his *teenage* ex-girlfriend. He's no loss to the planet."

*Oh-kay.*

Jason put a hand up. "Fine. You got this. I'll butt out."

J.J. said curtly, "Appreciated."

Jason checked his phone. Four thirty. Just enough time to squeeze in one more interview. "I think I'll try to speak to the Mayhew girl. Do you have an address on her?"

J.J. picked up his phone and texted the address. "I thought you were in a hurry to get to the newspaper archives?"

"The newspaper archives aren't going anywhere."

"That's not how you sounded this morning."

"I can't change what's in the archives."

"Huh?"

"Never mind. I'll start on the archives tomorrow."

"Okay. Whatever, I guess. You want me to come with you to interview Mayhew?"

Jason said casually, "No. I think you're turning up some very useful stuff. You should keep working this angle."

"Suit yourself." J.J. looked down at his laptop.

* * * * *

It wasn't hard to see how Terry "Baby" Mayhew, Quilletta's daughter, got her nickname.

Despite being nearly forty, she looked like a baby. Or maybe a toddler, would be more accurate. She was chubby, with a heart-shaped face, close-cut dark curls, wide-brown eyes, and a perfect set of dimples.

Also, given the way she recoiled when Jason showed his ID, a guilty conscience.

"I can't talk to you without a lawyer present," she said in alarm, and tried to close the front door.

"Wait a minute." Jason caught the door and held it in place. "Mrs. Mayhew, you're not in any trouble. I can't think of any good reason you would refuse to even speak with me."

Baby hesitated and then opened the door.

"Thanks. This won't take long, I promise," Jason said.

"My husband's going to be home soon."

"I'll keep that in mind."

Reluctantly, Baby led the way down an almost eerily unblemished hall to a living room that looked like it had been decorated by Mr. Clean. White walls, white carpet, white furniture, white blinds. Jason had seen operating rooms with more color—and warmth.

She waved Jason to take one of the spotless white chairs, positioning herself behind the sofa. As she warily watched him sit, he wondered if he was the chair's first occupant.

"Did you want something?" she asked grudgingly. "Tea? Coffee?"

"Just information." Jason smiled. He usually got good results with that smile, but Baby was not having any of it.

"I don't know why you have to come here," she burst out. "I don't know *anything*. I wasn't involved."

"Involved in what?" Jason inquired.

"Involved in anything. I wasn't even alive when Great-Uncle Roy sent those things home from the war."

"Which things are we talking about?" Jason asked.

She threw him a frightened look. "The things you were asking Mommy and Uncle Bert about."

Yeesh. Baby and now Mommy. That was kind of squicky, as his fourteen-year-old niece Nora would say.

He'd have loved to get Sam's take on this cast of characters.

"Could you describe some of those things for me?"

"No." She amended, "I don't know what things Great-Uncle Roy brought back and what was just...his."

"Sure. Did he bring a lot of things back?"

She swallowed. "I don't know. Why are you asking me?"

"You're mentioned in your great-uncle's will, so it seems like he was fond of you. And we know from talking to other people that he was a generous and thoughtful man."

"He was!"

"So it seems like he might have let you choose something from his art collection."

Bull's-eye.

She had been about to sit, but that had her back on her feet, looking terror-stricken. "He never did!"

"Okay," Jason said easily. "He never did. What was your great-uncle like?"

"I-I don't know what you're getting at."

Hm. What did she think he was getting at?

Jason smiled. "It's not a trick question. I didn't get to meet him, so it's hard to know what he was really like. I have to rely on other people's impressions."

"Oh." She smiled suddenly and sat down. "He was wonderful. Very artistic. And he always had funny stories to tell. He was very cultured too. He had been to Europe."

"You mean after the war?"

"Yes. A few times."

"Did you ever meet any of his friends?"

The defensive look was back on her face. "I don't care about any of that. He was wonderful to me."

Okay. *Now* he got it.

"Your great-uncle was gay. Is that correct?"

"It's no one's business!"

"I agree. Did your uncle—sorry, your great-uncle—did he ever mention the name Emerson Harley to you?"

She shook her head, and her curls bounced.

"I'm sure by now you're aware that your mother and your uncle attempted to sell three works of art from your great-uncle's collection, and that those paintings turned out to have been part of a trove of art and other objects stolen by the Nazis."

She nodded. "They didn't know that," she whispered.

"Of course not. Are you aware of any other items in your late great-uncle's art collection that he might have acquired around the same time?"

She quickly shook her head.

"Do you know if your mother and your uncle are intending to sell other items from your great-uncle's art collection?"

She opened her mouth, hesitated. "There *isn't* anything else," she insisted.

Jason sighed. "Mrs. Mayhew, Terry, I want to caution you about making false statements to a federal investigator."

Baby gave him a deer-in-the-headlights look—and another of those jerky swallows.

"You're not in any trouble right now, and presumably you'd like to keep it that way. So, let me give you a piece of advice. Either answer honestly, or decline to answer—which, yes, is going to tell me some of what I need to know—but don't lie to me. You won't like how that turns out, and you won't be doing your mother or uncle any good."

She licked her lips, started to speak.

He heard the floorboard, tensed, and turned before the loud "What the hell is going on here?" came from the doorway behind them.

Baby jumped. "Gary!"

"What are you doing, Terry?"

"I'm— This is the FBI."

"I know it's the goddamned FBI. Don't say a word to him."

"Mr. Mayhew?" Jason rose, getting his ID out. "I'm Special Agent—"

"That's right. I'm Terry's husband, and I don't give a fuck who you are, Special Agent Suit. I want you out of our house now."

"Really?" Jason said. "That's the way you want to play this?"

"You're goddamned right it's the way I want to play it. Unless you've got a warrant, get out of my house."

Jason unhurriedly opened his wallet, pulled out his card, handed his card to Baby. "Terry, if you change your mind, you can call me anytime."

She stared at the card like she thought it was a one-way ticket to the Big House, but then took it with trembling fingers.

"She's not going to change her mind," Mayhew said as Jason walked past him. He followed Jason down the sterile test-tube of a hallway to the front door.

Jason stepped onto the tiled Spanish-style porch. "I'm not sure what you're so afraid of," he said, "but it sure raises some red flags."

Mayhew slammed the door in his face.

# CHAPTER TEN

De Haan was not answering his phone.

Jason left a message letting him know he'd spoken to Terry Mayhew, then grabbed his copy of Karl Schütz's *Vermeer. The Complete Works*, asked the hotel front desk for some restaurant recs, and headed out to have dinner.

He was used to eating on his own. He actually preferred a good book to dinner with Russell, who never stopped talking sports scores, debating the merits of current girlfriends, or bitching about wasting his best years trailing after Jason on ACT investigations—though in fairness, Russell had eased up a bit on the job complaints in the last month.

He settled on a Mexican restaurant within walking distance of the hotel, ordered tacos with rice and beans, and—remembering Sam's concerns—diet Coke, and spent a surprisingly relaxing couple of hours reading and occasionally eating.

The Schütz book was beautifully produced and meticulously researched. All thirty-four of the artist's universally accepted paintings were included, along with gorgeous color plates reproducing every brushstroke, hue, detail, angle, and gesture contained in his paintings. There were even several large foldouts, which Jason did not dare expose to the risk of flying salsa.

Vermeer was a mystery in his own right, down to the exact date of his birth. There was no record of his apprenticeship, leading to the theory—however unlikely—that he was self-taught. But maybe the theory wasn't so unlikely given how extraordinary and unique his work was—not just precise, not just luminous, but almost inhumanly beautiful. In fact, another theory—dismissed by Schütz—was that Vermeer had used a camera obscura to obtain his hypnagogic results.

What Jason found especially amazing about the quality of universality in Vermeer's work was that Vermeer painted mostly domestic interior scenes of 17th century Dutch life. What was it about these paintings that so resonated with 21st century viewers? The bulk of his work, certainly the work of his peak years, was set in two smallish rooms in his house in Delft. Again and again, the paintings showed the same furniture and decorations in various arrangements, and Vermeer frequently portrayed the same people. Mostly women.

In fact, the only two paintings—the only two surviving paintings—with solitary male figures as their protagonists were a pair of later works titled *The Astronomer* and *The Geographer.* Or at least that's what they were called now. Back in 1713, they had been auctioned as *A work depicting a Mathematical Artist* and *A ditto by the Same Name*, demonstrating Vermeer's gift for really awful titles.

Another interesting point about the two paintings—Jason's favorites out of Vermeer's entire body of work—was that although one had been done in 1668 and the second in 1669, the same man had posed for them. One theory was that the man was Vermeer himself. Another theory was that it was his friend and estate executor, the noted microbiologist Antonie van Leeuwenhoek. Maybe. The fact remained, a slender man in his late thirties with long dark hair and a solemn face had posed for Vermeer as the painter worked on the two possibly thematically paired pictures.

So if *A Gentleman Washing His Hands in a Perspectival Room with Figures, Artful and Rare* did exist, it would be all the more, well, artful and rare.

Schütz had nothing to add on the topic of *A Gentleman Washing His Hands*. There was no question the painting had existed, but for it to have shown up in the tunnels of Engelshofen Castle, it would have had to survive two world wars and a whole lot of history.

That didn't mean it was impossible.

After dinner, Jason walked back to his hotel.

It was nearly dark by then, a warm summer's evening with lights winking on everywhere—some of those twinkles turning out to be fireflies. A cool breeze, flavored with clear summer air and wide-open plains, dusted the sidewalks and stirred leaves and flags and imaginatively painted hanging signs. The sidewalks were crowded, but strangers smiled when you caught their gaze. He could hear distant music playing and the faraway, mournful wail of a train.

Bozwin was a college town. A pretty town too, sheltered in the blue-black shadows of the Bridger Range, and effort had gone into keeping it that way. There was a variety of archi-tecture—Art Deco, Italianate, and Mission Revival—but one thing every style had in common was the effort made to pre-serve and protect. He liked that. And there was plenty of shop-ping, plenty of places to eat and drink. It was a nice place to visit, no question.

Though he couldn't help thinking there was a real lack of ethnic or cultural diversity. And despite that surprisingly well-connected airport, this was a very long way from pretty much everywhere he needed to be.

He had stopped to look in the window of a closed art gallery when he caught the reflection of a police SUV. He glanced around, recognized Chief Sandford's silvery hair and blunt features beneath a baseball cap.

The chief was looking straight ahead and didn't seem to see him, which was fine with Jason. Local law enforcement didn't always welcome the Bureau with open arms, but he'd rarely had such a hostile reception.

And he was still curious as to why Bert Thompson's first instinct had been to call the Bozwin police chief after the shootout at his ranch. Maybe the chief was a personal friend of the family, though he hadn't seemed particularly chummy with Bert.

When he reached his hotel, Jason got out his laptop and settled down to work. That was usually how he spent his evenings on the road.

If Sam had had the evening off, it might have been nice to walk around town and catch some of the summer activities he had seen advertised on posters and flyers: a local theater was running classic Westerns, the Montana State University was doing Shakespeare in the Park, and on Main Street the summer music festival was in full swing.

But they weren't on vacation, and he had reports to write up.

He was doing his best to keep a careful and accurate account of his investigation, making particular effort to be scrupulous in any and all matters related to Emerson Harley's potential involvement.

When the time came to turn in his final case report—and regardless of his findings—he intended to make full disclosure about his personal connection to Emerson Harley. He knew his chief at the ACT, Karan Kapszukiewicz, was not going to be happy. At all. And George Potts, his supervisor at the LA Field Office, would be even less pleased. There was a good chance he was going to receive a letter of censure for his file. That would be hard to take.

Not least because a letter of censure put him in danger of losing a much coveted spot on the highly competitive Art Crime Team.

He hoped not. He didn't *think* that would happen, but he couldn't be sure. Even knowing the risk, he felt he had to pursue the path he had started down on.

There was another possibility too: that he would be fired outright. But *that* he refused to even think about.

Accordingly, he noted Quilletta's allegations that her uncle had been ordered to take the artwork by a commanding officer, and de Haan's conviction that MFAA Deputy Chief Emerson Harley was the best and most likely candidate for Captain Roy Thompson's accomplice.

He also noted that neither Terry Mayhew nor Edgar Roberts had recognized Harley's name or remembered hearing Thompson mention him, but so far, the scales were not tilting in his favor. Still, it was early in the investigation.

He was hoping spending some quality time in the *Bozwin Daily Chronicle*'s archives might turn up the names of some other potential suspects, although if de Haan hadn't identified them by now, they probably did not exist.

By the time he finished writing up his notes and checking and answering emails, following up current cases as best he could long-distance, it was after ten. Still no word from Sam.

Not looking too promising, then.

He tried to do a bit more research on *A Gentleman Washing His Hands*, but there really did not seem to be any more to discover.

He did come across a fanciful reconstruction of the legendary lost work painted by Delft artist Arthur Stam in 2013 and displayed at the Delft art gallery Ruimte Remmelink in spring of that year. The painting was...well, it was not Vermeer, of course.

It was an interesting experiment, though. Jason studied the recreated room and small, pudgy central figure intently. Putting aside technique, palette, composition, and Vermeer's apparent sorcery, it seemed to him that Stam entirely missed the point, for lack of a better word, of Vermeer's work.

Stam had tackled the lost painting again, this time in a three-dimensional installation. And, in Jason's opinion, he'd got it even more wrong. Vermeer had not simply painted scenes of comfortable domesticity; he had tried to convey a quality of life, even perhaps the very essence of civilization. There was something profound in Vermeer's work. Somehow the simplicity of the scenes he chose to portray only underlined their importance, their sublimity. Vermeer seemed to be illustrating what it meant to be human.

But then in Stam's efforts to recreate Vermeer's lost work, he too was illustrating what it meant to be human.

At eleven, his cell phone rang. Jason picked up, assuming it was Sam, but the screen showed de Haan's number.

"Hi, this is West."

It was kind of late for phone calls, but he didn't think much of it until he heard a garbled static background noise followed by a high-pitched...Jason didn't even know how to describe it. Something between the sound of accidentally dialing a fax machine and falling over a metal trash barrel.

"*Hans?*"

The line went dead.

Jason pressed Redial.

The call rang and rang and then went to messages.

What the hell had that been about?

A mistake obviously. Maybe de Haan had butt-dialed him?

Jason yawned, considered making coffee—shuddered—and went back to scouring the Internet.

He found one more still earlier three-dimensional reconstruction by Stam, which was at least closer thematically to Vermeer's usual work, along with a short video on the making of the viewing cabinet. In Stam's words, this first attempt was: "The dreamed painting, entirely in the spirit of Vermeer, without a trace of a 20th century personality."

Uh, sure.

No question, *A Gentleman Washing His Hands* had fired creative imaginations for centuries.

Partly that was due to the small body of exquisite work Vermeer had left behind. There were various theories on why Vermeer had produced so few paintings during his short lifetime. He had worked slowly, painstakingly, and despite Schütz's argument, a convincing case could be made as to his possible use of a camera obscura, which would have slowed the process even more. He preferred to use very expensive pigments but was not wealthy, so probably had trouble obtaining the materials he required. And being unable to support his wife and eleven children with his painting, he had a day job as an art dealer and innkeeper. He was also kept busy as head of the Guild of Saint Luke, a local trade association for paintings.

Though moderately successful during his lifetime, Vermeer died deeply in debt, and for nearly two centuries following his passing, was virtually forgotten. It wasn't until the 19th century that his work had been rediscovered and the insatiable demand began.

If the Nazis had stumbled across that Vermeer in a private collection, they would have known exactly what they had. Whole organizations were devoted to looting and stealing the world's cultural treasures. Much of the treasure of Engelshofen Castle had been earmarked for Hitler's own Führermuseum.

From that perspective, it made sense that if the painting existed, it would have been found at Engelshofen.

When his cell phone buzzed beneath his head, it was after one. Jason jumped, pressed Accept, and Sam said, "I know you said to call, but it's late and we're both beat, so if you want to go back to sleep…"

Jason swallowed his disappointment. "Yeah, of course. If that's what you prefer."

"What I'd prefer is for you to open your door so we can go back to sleep together."

Jason jumped up, threw open the door, and Sam, heavy-eyed and hair mussed, stepped inside.

Jason hugged him. "Hi. Why didn't you just knock?"

"I didn't want to wake your neighbors. You're a heavy sleeper, West." Sam kissed him—and then kissed him again. "I could hear you snoring all the way out in the hall." He was undressing as they walked.

Jason kissed him back, leading him toward the bed strewn with his laptop, notes, and book. He scrambled to clear the mattress, pulled back the comforter, and Sam, by that point wearing only a pair of navy-blue briefs, crashed down.

Jason turned out the overhead light, turned out the bed-side lamp, and crawled into bed beside Sam.

Sam wrapped his arm around him, pulled him snug, buried his face in Jason's hair, and promptly went to sleep.

# CHAPTER ELEVEN

He woke to the sound of sex.

Loud and energetic sex.

His first horrified thought was that Russell and Martinez were doing it.

In the hotel walls.

Or maybe on the window ledge.

Somewhere nearby. The noise was muffled but uncomfortably close. And it went on and on.

*Jesus, would they please just hurry it up?*

He stiffened in astonishment at the distinct and sudden sound of flapping wings.

Straight sex really *was* different.

He raised his head, blinking.

"What's up?" Sam mumbled, eyes still closed.

"Do you hear that?"

"Hm?"

They were silent for a moment. Jason wasn't sure if Sam hadn't drifted back to sleep.

Sam said finally, sleepily, "Pigeons," and heaved onto his front, half burying his face in his pillow.

"*Pigeons?* Seriously?"

The hotel's sex-crazed pigeons continued to go at it like… er, pigeons, it turned out, all the while making those distractingly human sounds.

"It sounds like they're…" He trailed off as the bird—one of the birds?—seemed to reach a full-throated crescendo. "For God's sake. Tell me that doesn't sound like somebody in the next room has a-a prostitute with him!"

Sam's shoulders began to jerk. He made a smothered *woofing* sound in the pillows.

Jason threw him a distracted look. "I mean, I've never known California pigeons to act like that."

Sam started to wheeze like Muttley the cartoon dog. He rolled onto his side and pulled Jason over.

"You've led a sheltered life, West."

"Not so much."

"I don't know what's funnier. Your outrage at avian sex or that you immediately leap to the idea a man would have to resort to a prostitute—"

Jason started laughing. "I'm not *outraged*—"

"I see. Then you do consider dial-a-hooker to be standard operating practice?"

He didn't laugh often and rarely hard, so it was a pleasure—Jason was smiling—watching Sam's eyes crinkle and that little peek of teeth.

"No. Well, whatever. But I mean, *listen* to that," Jason insisted. By now he was just trying to win another laugh out of Sam. "I wouldn't be surprised if we saw a bunch of feathers blow out of the air vents."

Sam laughed again. "I wish we had more time. I'd like to ruffle *your* feathers, West."

"Mmm." That would be nice. No lie.

As though reading his thoughts, Sam said, "This is nice. I like waking up to you."

Jason assented. "We should do it more often."

"We should." Sam merely sounded regretful now, like they both knew there was no chance of that. And, of course, they did both know that.

For a minute or so they held each other, breathing in quiet unison, not speaking, not moving. Then Sam exhaled, raised his head, and peered at the clock.

He growled.

"Time?" Jason asked.

"We're late." He dropped a kiss on Jason's forehead, sat up, and retrieved his clothes.

Jason sat up too, then walked into the bathroom. He turned on his toothbrush, listening for Sam's answer as he called, "What have you got planned for tonight?"

"Nothing so far." That could change, of course, and Sam added, "I'll let you know." Now dressed—mostly—he stepped into the bathroom, and Jason turned off his toothbrush.

Sam kissed him. "Minty fresh." He wiped a bit of foam from his lip and said, "Be careful out there."

"You know me."

"I do, so be careful, West."

"Back at you, Kennedy."

Jason stared at his reflection, listening for the sound of the closing door, and then sighed.

*     *     *     *     *

Once again, he beat J.J. down to breakfast. While he drank his coffee, he tried phoning de Haan.

No reply.

This time he couldn't even leave a message. Instead, he got the dreaded *the customer you are trying to reach is unavailable.*

It seemed a little odd. Was de Haan angry about something? He didn't seem like a guy who would hesitate to speak his mind, if that was the case. He had not been happy with Jason the day before, but they had still been on speaking terms.

At this point, de Haan needed them more than they needed him. So again, odd.

J.J. arrived a minute later, grabbed a coffee and a Cinnabon, and said, "Head 'em up and move 'em out, West."

"Yeah, I've been waiting for *you*," Jason said, but he was talking to his partner's back.

They passed Travis Petty on his way into the hotel. Petty, looking handsome as hell in a navy suit with a rose-colored— *Jesus, rose-colored?*—tie nodded gravely in greeting.

"Hey," Jason said.

"Hey," Petty returned in that same expressionless voice.

"I don't like that guy's tie," J.J. said as they got in the rental car.

Jason laughed and started the engine.

On the short ride to the office, J.J. said, "I know it's none of my business, but Mari was telling me last night that Kennedy and Petty used to be pretty cozy."

It probably wasn't J.J.'s business, and he probably shouldn't listen to this, but Jason said, "Mari? Is that Martinez?"

"Yeah. For Marianna." J.J. paused to take a bite of Cinnabon. "Their whatever-it-was was widely enough known that you and Kennedy are now the main topic of office gossip."

"Clearly."

J.J. shrugged that off. "Petty is their golden boy. He was almost named Supervisory Agent over James Salazar, which, given Salazar's seniority…"

If he and J.J. had reached the point where J.J. was sharing office gossip, their partnership had come a long way. Jason didn't like hearing any of this, let alone discussing it, but he said neutrally, "I appreciate your looking out for me. Sam told me about Petty the night he arrived."

"Did he?" J.J. sounded both relieved and a little surprised.

Jason nodded. He searched around for a change of subject. "How's it going with Martinez?"

J.J. threw him an odd look. Why?

It occurred to Jason that he had never actually initiated a personal conversation with J.J. In fact, he'd tried to avoid any such conversations. J.J. was a pretty vocal guy about his likes and dislikes—most of which they did not share—and Jason preferred his own thoughts most of the time. But, well, there was no denying this trip had made a difference in their work relationship, maybe even moved it forward a square or two on the gameboard.

J.J. said gloomily, "She doesn't want to move."

"You *asked* her? Already?"

"Of course not. Not directly. But we were talking in generalities last night. Her mom is disabled and her dad is quite a bit older—late seventies. She's got brothers and sisters, a *lot* of brothers and sisters, but they've all got their own families, so a lot of the responsibility for the parents has fallen on Mari."

"Right."

"Plus, she *likes* Montana." J.J. sounded disbelieving.

Jason admitted, "Sam likes Montana."

They were both silent.

"I mean, it *is* beautiful," Jason said. You couldn't argue that with those towering mountain ranges and breathtaking blue skies bearing down on them.

J.J. made a skeptical sound.

They glanced at each other and shared reluctant, pained smiles.

**M**ore bad news waited for them at the Resident Agency.

"Brody Stevens's parents are filing a wrongful-death suit," SAC Phillips announced after bringing them into her office.

"How the hell do they figure that?" Jason asked.

J.J. was stone silent.

"Don't shoot the messenger. I'm just informing you of the newest developments. No one from this team was involved in the incident. This does not actually concern the Bozwin RA."

"That's an unusual perspective," Jason said.

She gave him a cool, unfriendly look. Yep, she definitely did not like him.

"Jesus Christ," J.J. said. "Where does this leave us? I'm the guy who shot the kid."

"A lot depends on the SIRG's findings." She grimly regarded his stunned expression, then relented. "I don't think you have anything to worry about, Agent Russell. There are plenty of witnesses to corroborate your version of events. Even Stevens's cousin initially backed up your account. He's since recanted, but..." She shrugged. "That said, the sooner you two finish your investigation and get the hell out of Dodge, the easier life will be for all of us."

"I'm heading down to the newspaper morgue," Jason told J.J. when they were back in their own office.

J.J. didn't answer.

Jason glanced at him. "Russell?"

J.J. threw him a distracted look. "What?"

"I'll be down at the *Bozwin Daily Chronicle* if you need me—" He broke off as J.J. grabbed his phone and started tapping the keypad.

"I'm calling my lawyer. Which is what you should be doing."

"Right. Well, when you finish phoning your lawyer—"

J.J.'s head jerked up. He glared at Jason. "Do you not *get* it, West? Our careers are *over*. I shot a *kid*. I killed a *kid*."

Jason closed the office door. "I was there. You also saved lives. Maybe mine included. He was armed with an assault weapon."

"*He was a kid.*"

Jason was silent. Was J.J. really fearing for his career, or was this something else? Or was it both? Jason had a feeling it was all of the above. Whatever it was, and cold-blooded though it might be, they—he—didn't have time to deal with it. The clock was ticking—and this clock was attached to a time bomb.

"Do you think there's something you should have—could have—done differently? You couldn't talk to him. We're not trained to shoot the guns out of people's hands. I can't see that we had any other choice."

"It's not *we*, West. *You* didn't kill anyone."

"That's the luck of the draw. Literally, the luck of the draw. It could just as easily have been me."

"Yeah, but it wasn't." J.J. put his phone down, put his head in his hands. "Why did he have to be a fucking *kid*?"

"I don't know." Jason sighed and pulled out the chair facing J.J.'s. "I wish it hadn't gone down the way it did. But I'm not sorry that we're alive."

J.J. groaned. "When I saw how fucking young he was…" He squeezed his head tighter. "I almost threw up."

"I know." He had been shocked to see how young Duane Jones was, but that had braced him for the worst when he'd looked at Brody Stevens's body. "And I know this doesn't make it better, but it's because of your actions that more people weren't injured or killed." He reached over and gave J.J.'s shoulder a hard, comforting squeeze. Straight out of the Sam Kennedy playbook.

J.J. sat up, dragged the heels of his hands against the corners of his eyes. "Yeah." He gave Jason a quick, awkward look. "If you're going to spend the day going through microfilm or whatever, you ought to get going."

"Right." He hesitated.

"Will you *go*?" J.J. said impatiently.

"Going."

"Hey, West—"

Jason glanced back.

J.J. grimaced.

Jason rolled his eyes and opened the door—and nearly walked into Sam.

Sam was looking dapper—if grim—in his second favorite suit, a gray sharkskin.

"Can I talk to you a minute?" he said.

His expression, his tone... Not good. Jason's nerves yanked tight. He made sure his voice sounded calm when he replied, "Of course."

Did this have to do with the lawsuit? Or was it something else? Could Sam have—had he possibly found out that Emerson Harley was a suspect in Jason's stolen art case?

Sam turned and led the way down the hall to an empty office. Well, not empty, because his phone and briefcase lay on the desk. That was Sam's version of making himself at home.

Jason stepped inside the office, and Sam closed the door.

Jason's unease mounted. "What is it? What's going on?"

Sam let out a long, quiet breath. "I just got word from the RCMP. It looks like—" He stopped and corrected himself. "There is a strong possibility that Dr. Jeremy Kyser is dead."

# CHAPTER TWELVE

The relief was instantaneous and almost overwhelming.

*Thank God. Thank God. Thank God.*

For a moment he couldn't think beyond that sense of freedom, of deliverance. Jason's knees felt weak, he almost dropped into the chair before the desk, but then he absorbed the expression—the lack of expression—on Sam's face, took in the measuring way Sam was watching him.

Sam, who understood better than anyone how much strain Jason was under—and who had probably formed a clinical opinion on how much more Jason could take.

Jason matched his tone to Sam's unemotional timbre. "You don't think it's true."

Sam said at once, "I don't know if it's true. The recovered body is too damaged to identify without DNA testing, and DNA testing is going to take a while."

Jason nodded automatically. "What happened? How was he found?"

"He appears to have been renting a boat under an assumed name in Lunenburg, Nova Scotia."

"He was still in Canada." Jason was trying to process.

"Apparently so."

"What happened?"

"The investigation is ongoing. The boat was discovered on fire yesterday evening. A badly burned body was located in the main cabin, along with a partially charred passport, wallet, and other items identifying the victim as Jeremy Kyser."

"It's too convenient," Jason said.

Apparently, this was the deduction Sam wanted from him because he seemed to relax slightly.

"Maybe."

"He's covering his tracks."

"It's possible. Kyser has incentive to disappear, and a death which results in a body that can't easily be identified is, as you say, pretty convenient."

"What happens next?"

*He's coming for me.*

The paralyzing thought flew into Jason's brain. He managed not to say it aloud.

"Because of the special circumstances, they'll try to expedite the DNA testing, and then we'll see where we are." Sam said carefully, "It's not bad news."

"I don't believe—and you don't believe—it's good news."

"We don't know what it is. Yet. We will."

Jason nodded. Because what else could he do?

For one *halle-fucking-lujah* of a moment he had thought it was over, and the relief had been…almost embarrassing. But it wasn't over, and coming so close to deliverance merely made this part harder.

So he nodded again. "Okay. Thanks for the heads-up."

Sam made a move toward him. "Jason—"

He managed a twitchy smile and stepped back. He could not afford to accept comfort, sympathy, at this point. "I'm okay. It's better if I just get back to work. I need to focus on something else right now."

The concerned understanding in Sam's gaze almost undid him. Sam said gruffly, reluctantly, "All right, West."

\* \* \* \* \*

It turned out visiting the *Bozwin Daily Chronicle* had been a good call. Only the year 1926 had been digitized and was available online. The earliest years of the paper had been put on microfilm, but budget or interest had waned after 1935. Jason spent several hours poring over bound volumes of newspapers, starting his search with June 1944.

He hit pay dirt a few weeks' worth of papers later, when Captain Roy Thompson wrote to his parents and siblings, describing the Normandy landing.

*You can't imagine the amazing sight of these tracers going up into the sky. The underbelly of clouds turned red like charred embers, a mass of red death to any plane within the circle of our anti-aircraft fire. It was a beautiful sight from our point of view, but a kind of beauty only a soldier can understand.*

It was fascinating—and a little disconcerting—to read Thompson's own words. Jason had not expected his thief to be so literate or lyrical. That was not common of the crooks he typically dealt with.

In January of 1945, Thompson wrote:

*There's a lot of snow on the Western Front these days, and the country looks like a Christmas card. The trees are like old queens stooping from under the weight of their ermine robes. The wires loop from pole to pole like tinsel on a Christmas tree, except where the weight of the ice and snow has pulled them down and the signal repairmen are patching them. Snow lies smooth on the hillsides—it's beautiful. But I also have seen plenty of action and have just about had my fill. It's pretty tough to take seeing some of your buddies getting knocked off; especially the ones who sweated it out together away, back in our training days.*

He did not want to like this guy, did not want to feel sympathy for him. What Thompson had done was unconscionable, and then he'd made it worse by dragging Jason's grandfather into it. But there was no question Thompson had gone through hell—or that he made an engaging narrator.

At noon, Jason took a break. He was not hungry, but his eyes were ready to fall out of his head. He needed to stretch his legs and smell something besides disintegrating pulp and ink.

He walked over to a small café and purchased an iced-coffee smoothie, which he drank on the patio while checking his phone messages.

Still nothing from de Haan.

Jason clicked on Contacts, clicked on de Haan's name, waited for the phone to ring—and got nothing. Not even a message saying de Haan was not available.

Dead silence.

He hung up, tried again, and listened to that absolute void of sound with a bad feeling in the pit of his stomach. Why the hell was de Haan's phone dead?

Even if de Haan had decided to leave the country—and no way would he give up that easily—he wouldn't have gone radio silent. He and Jason had been speaking regularly for over a month. De Haan would not fly off in a huff, and even if he did, he would not stop communicating with Jason while so much of the case was still up in the air.

Something was not right.

He should have recognized it sooner, but he'd had so much on his mind that it had been only too easy to set aside de Haan's uncharacteristic quiet as something to be dealt with later. But that was his mistake, because considered in connection with that strange hang-up call the night before—the call he had dismissed as a misdial—something was seriously off.

He phoned J.J.

"Have you heard from de Haan?"

J.J., sounding back to his normal self, said disinterestedly, "He's your pen pal, not mine."

"I haven't heard from him since I spoke to him yesterday afternoon."

"Count your blessings."

"I'm heading over to Big Sky Motor Lodge to check on him."

"If you want my advice, West, leave sleeping Dutchmen lie."

"Yeah. I'll be in touch." Jason disconnected and went to find his car.

\* \* \* \* \*

De Haan's blue compact sat in the back of the parking lot of Big Sky Motor Lodge.

Jason's heart sank when he spotted the familiar vehicle. It seemed to confirm his worst suspicions. And yet his worst suspicions made no sense.

He parked, got out of his car, and went to the frostily air-conditioned front office.

A gangling twentysomething scrolling through a—given the panicked way he clicked out and rolled his chair back from the computer screen—porn site, greeted him.

"Hey! Hi there! Welcome to the Big Sky Motor Lodge. What can I do you for?"

"Do you have a guest by the name of Hans de Haan staying with you?"

The kid's freckled brow wrinkled. "The German guy?"

"Dutch. Is he still staying here?"

"Uh, I think so. I just got on duty."

Jason showed his ID. "Can you ring his room, please?"

The clerk goggled over his ID and threw Jason a worried look. "Uh, sure. What did he do?"

"This is just a welfare check," Jason said, as if the FBI went around verifying health and safety as part of their everyday duties.

"Sure, sure." The kid picked up the phone and dialed de Haan's room. Jason could hear ringing on the other end. He watched the kid glance uneasily out the front window at the row of upper-story rooms.

"I don't think he's in," the kid said.

"His car's in the parking lot."

"Oh. Well, maybe he…" The kid trailed off at Jason's expression.

"I think we should check on him," Jason said.

"You do?"

Jason nodded.

The desk clerk replaced the handset reluctantly. "Maybe I should call my manager."

"You can call your manager after we check on your guest."

"Okay."

"Now would be good," Jason prompted.

"Right. Okay." The kid slid open a drawer, removed a key, and proceeded Jason out into the blinding sunlight. They crossed the parking lot and went up the steps to the second level.

Jason noted the security camera positioned under the eaves at the end of the walkway.

"Does that work?" he asked.

"Uh, no. It's just supposed to be a deterrent."

"It would be more of a deterrent if it actually worked."

The clerk had no response. They continued, footsteps thumping hollowly, down the walkway to room 224.

The drapes were drawn across the front window. The room's air conditioner hummed noisily. A *Do not Disturb* placard hung on the door.

"*Oh,*" said the clerk hopefully. "Maybe he doesn't want to talk to anyone."

Jason ignored him. He thumped on the dingy orange door—an official side of the fist bang to the face of the door. The Do Not Disturb fell off the knob and landed at their feet.

No response from within de Haan's room, but the maid doing the next room hastily rolled her cart down the open walkway, where she watched nervously from a safe distance.

"Maybe he's not in there," the kid said. "Maybe he walked out to grab some lunch."

"Maybe." Jason pulled out his cell phone and rang de Haan.

He wasn't really expecting an answer. De Haan's phone had appeared to be dead earlier, but as they stood there silently waiting, de Haan's cell started ringing from inside the room.

Jason swore quietly. He glanced at the clerk, who was watching him with wide eyes. "I need you to open the door and then stand aside."

The kid hesitated, read Jason's expression, and unlocked the door. His hands were shaking.

"That's great. I'll take it from here." The clerk didn't budge. Jason moved him to the side, and pushed the door open. "Hans?" he called.

It took his eyes a second or two to adjust to the dimness, but he didn't need to see the motionless form on the bed to know the worst. His stomach rose in instinctive protest at the smell rolling out of the room.

Even the kid knew what that was.

He gulped. "Oh no! Is he *dead*?"

Jason nodded, found his voice. "Yeah. Call 911."

For a moment the kid just stared at him, chest rising and falling, and then he stumbled away and ran down the walkway, his sneakers soundless as a ghost's as he sprinted away.

Jason let his head fall back, drew a deep breath.

*Shit. Shit. Shit.*

How the hell— No, *why* the hell had this happened?

It made no sense.

Zero sense.

Unless… Why was he assuming that de Haan had met with foul play? Maybe it was a natural death. That wasn't out of the question. De Haan was a middle-aged guy under a lot of stress, with a fondness for steak sandwiches. Maybe he'd had a stroke or a heart attack. These things happened a lot more frequently than murder.

Jason felt for his gloves. He slipped them on and stepped into the gloomy interior of the room. He took a moment to scan the layout of the possible crime scene, to consciously absorb his first impressions.

TV and lights were off. Air conditioner was cranked. De Haan's cell phone rested on the table beside the bed. It was plugged in and charging.

A suitcase lay open on a wooden luggage stand, its contents neatly folded. De Haan's closed laptop sat on the desk.

No obvious signs of violence. No obvious signs of any disturbance at all.

Jason studied the floor around the bed. Nothing on the carpet indicated…anything. A pair of balled-up socks rested at the foot of the nightstand.

He approached the bed.

Hans lay face up on top of the neatly made spread. He was not wearing his spectacles but he was fully dressed, down to his shoes and socks. The shoulders and front of his shirt were soaked with blood. The blood was brown and completely dried.

"What the hell, Hans…"

Jason bent down. Even without turning on the lamp, he could see part of the ghastly wound on the top of de Haan's skull and deduced most of the damage had been done from behind.

He touched de Haan's wrist. His skin was ice cold, advanced rigor was present, fixed lividity, the corneas of his eyes were cloudy. Jason straightened, stepped back from the bed, and considered.

You didn't have to be a forensics expert to tell de Haan had been dead several—probably between six to eight—hours. He remembered yesterday evening's phone call, which he'd dismissed as a misdial. That had come in around eleven, but then taking into account the temperature of this room… Yeah, maybe you did need to be a forensics expert.

He could still draw a few conclusions from this crime-scene-that-was-not-a-crime-scene.

Obviously, de Haan had not been in bed when he'd been attacked. No attempt had been made to stage the death scene. Had he even been in the room? Highly doubtful.

Where the hell had he been, then?

Jason squatted down and studied the well-worn soles of de Haan's tennis shoes. It looked like bits of green-black something were stuck to the welt. Weeds? Moss? Grass? Again, not his area of expertise.

Their best bet would be to access his phone records to see if his cell had pinged off any nearby towers, but that would take time and a court order. And, despite the fact that de Haan had been his complainant, there was no *their*. This was not going to be Jason's case. This homicide would go to local law enforcement.

Jason's gaze fell on the framed photo of a smiling blonde woman in an oval rosewood frame. That had to be Anna, the art teacher who was waiting for Hans to finish chasing his lost treasure and settle down so they could raise a child together.

His stomach knotted. He shook off the reaction impatiently. De Haan had not been afraid to take risks. If he had known the potential cost of his quest, it was highly probable he would have kept right on. He had not been deterred by the shootout at Thompson's ranch.

Even so, art historian was not supposed to be a dangerous profession.

But *was* de Haan's death linked to his search for the Engelshofen Castle treasure?

His laptop was still there. His phone was still there. And now that the federal government was involved, the investigation he had initiated would not stop with his death.

Jason turned to study the room a final time and noticed the thin band of light beneath the bathroom door.

He drew his weapon, opened the door and, of course, despite the light left on, the small room was empty. There was a window over the toilet; one of those old-fashioned jalousies with glass slats—at least, judging by the remaining hardware. The slats and the strips of hardware had been removed, leaving a perfect empty square of an entrance. Not a large entrance. Though the window was wider than most found in motel bathrooms, it was probably not big enough to stuff a body through.

The sound of approaching sirens drifted through the opening.

Jason cast one last look around the bathroom, but there was nothing of note. Sink, toilet, and tub looked clean. De Haan had used baby shampoo, complimentary soap, and baking-soda toothpaste. The towels, including the ones crumpled on the floor, were bone dry, as was the used washcloth hanging over the shower-curtain bar.

Jason stepped out of the bathroom and froze. A black silhouette filled the door to the motel room. Even with sunlight shining in his eyes, Jason could make out the glint of metal buttons on a uniform and off the barrel of the weapon pointed at him.

The cop didn't speak, and something in that stark silence raised the hair on the back of Jason's neck. He knew without a shadow of a doubt that the man in the doorway was weighing whether to shoot him. He also knew without a shadow of a doubt who that man was.

"*Seriously?*" he said, and his voice shook. He was so furious, he almost forgot to be afraid. "You're pulling your gun on brother law enforcement? If you're aiming at me, you better pull the trigger, asshole."

"I saw his badge," the kid from the front desk said faintly from the landing.

After another second that lasted a year, the cop holstered his weapon.

"You're no brother of mine, jackass," Police Chief Sandford said. "What the hell are you doing in here?"

"You know goddamned well what I was doing in here," Jason snapped. He was still buzzing with adrenaline and mad as hell.

"I'll tell you what I know," Sandford said. "You don't have any business here. *You* know goddamned well you should have waited for us before you entered. So, if you don't want to be arrested for unlawful entry, interfering with a police investigation, tampering with evidence, and anything and everything else I can think of hitting you with, *get the hell off my crime scene.*"

# CHAPTER THIRTEEN

"**Y**ou really believe Sandford would have shot you if the desk clerk hadn't been watching?" Sam's tone was neutral, his gaze watchful.

"He was considering it. That I do believe." Jason swallowed his Kamikaze and set the shot glass on the table. Though he'd had several hours to process his close call, he still felt rattled.

They were eating dinner at the Club Tavern and Grill. Jason had figured Sam would like the dark, retro steakhouse vibe of the place, and he was right. As for himself, he didn't care where they went. He was too wound up to eat. As days went? First, there had been the news of the wrongful-death lawsuit, then word about Kyser, then his complainant had been murdered, and *then* he'd nearly been shot by a goddamned cop. Not a great day. Not his usual workday Wednesday.

Even having spent the last few hours finding out everything he could about Police Chief Sandford, Jason couldn't understand why things had nearly gone down the way they had that afternoon at the Big Sky Motor Lodge. Especially since there really didn't seem to be anything sinister in Sandford's personal or work history. Married twice—still married to the second wife—four kids, two in college, one mortgage, and the normal amount of debt for a guy in his position.

"That kid *had* to have told him I said I was an FBI agent."

"It seems probable."

"Which means he held that weapon on me knowing that in all likelihood I was another law-enforcement officer." It still made Jason's heart pound with anger and indignation remembering those horrifying seconds while Sandford had weighed whether to pull the trigger.

Sam said nothing.

"I'll be the first to admit, I'm a little touchy when guns are pointed in my direction," Jason said. "But something was going on there."

"You've got good instincts." Sam said it almost dismissively. "If you believe that was the situation, then I think you're likely right. What I don't understand is why."

"You mean what would be the motive for shooting me?"

"That, yes."

Was there another angle to this that Jason didn't see? Knowing the way Sam's brain worked, probably.

"I don't know. I've been trying to work that out all afternoon. I mean, he wasn't charmed the first time we met, but I don't think I gave him grounds to kill me."

Sam made a sound more pained than amused.

"He's been police chief for nearly ten years. His Yelp reviews aren't great, but no one has actually sued him."

"His...Yelp...reviews?"

"Yeah." Jason grinned. "Even FBI Field Offices get Yelp reviews. *You* probably have Yelp reviews."

"You're not kidding, are you?"

"Nope. Anyway, there seems to be some connection between Sandford and the Thompsons. After the shootout at Big Sky Guest Ranch—and I can't tell you how ridiculous I feel saying that aloud—Bert Thompson phoned Sandford, and despite the fact that the incident took place in another county, Sandford drove out there and tried to take control of the investigation."

Sam considered this and shrugged. "That could be nothing more than good old networking."

"Sure."

The waitress delivered another round of drinks and asked how they were enjoying their meals.

Jason glanced down at his salad. He didn't remember it arriving at the table. "Great," he said, and she continued on her mission of mercy, drinks tray held high.

"It's interesting, though." Sam sipped his whisky sour, considering. "But Sandford didn't last in his job this long by not knowing how things worked. He had to realize that shooting you would not stop any ongoing investigation into the Thompsons. In fact, it would probably accelerate things. So what would be the point?"

"What's the point in killing de Haan?" Jason asked. "The investigation into the stolen art doesn't end with his death. Not on his end and not on this end. The US government is involved now. There's no stopping this case driving to its natural conclusion."

"I agree." Sam studied him. "Do you think Sandford is somehow involved in de Haan's homicide?"

"I don't know. If he hadn't held that gun on me, I'd have said no chance in hell."

Sam said, "It's possible he didn't know who you were. It's possible the kid didn't give him the full story or that he didn't wait to hear the full story. It's possible he went into that situation with a set of biases we don't know about."

Sometimes Sam's dispassionate objectivity was aggravating, no lie. This was one of those times.

Jason said grudgingly, "True."

"It's also possible that the situation is exactly as you've described. We don't know the extent of his personal loyalties."

"Okay, yes, and here's another thing—" Jason broke off in surprise as Sam reached out to cover his hand.

"You need to eat something," Sam said quietly. His gaze was steady, serious. "You've had three drinks and nothing to eat."

Jason flushed, withdrew his hand. "I'm not drunk."

"I know you're not drunk. You need to eat. You've had a hell of a day, and you're running on empty. You can't do this on nervous energy alone—and you know that."

"Jesus," Jason muttered. He took a couple of bites of lettuce and steak, managed to swallow, managed not to throw it up, and after a perilous couple of seconds, did feel better.

He scowled at Sam, who continued to watch him in that grave, measuring way. Sam smiled faintly.

"You can thank me later."

"Uh, yeah, I wasn't actually thinking of thanking you."

Sam's grin turned a little wolfish. "Then I'll thank *you* later."

"Anyway, as I was saying, the Thompsons aren't in a bad position legally right now. They've reached a tentative agreement with the Aaldenberg van Apeldoorn Museum, the government's official position for now is that they are cooperating... I don't see that they have any motive for wanting to be rid of de Haan. Or me. And if they don't have a motive, why would Sandford have a motive?"

"That's my point," Sam said. "It's possible Sandford went into that situation with expectations we're unaware of."

"He was in stealth mode, that's another thing."

Sam made an inquiring sound.

"He arrived on scene Code 2, no lights, no siren. I'll guarantee it. He was there way before the rest of his team."

Sam shook his head. "There could be a lot of reasons for that."

Could there? Jason couldn't think of any offhand. De Haan's battered head and staring eyes flashed into his mind, and his stomach lurched. He wished he hadn't eaten. But no, Sam was right. He couldn't run forever on caffeine and booze, not if things were going to continue like today.

Maybe he should take up smoking.

"Something funny?" Sam inquired.

"No. Definitely not." He sighed and made himself eat a couple more bites. He was on the verge of getting smashed, and that would not be helpful.

Sam said, "So he threatened to arrest you, tossed you out of his crime scene—"

"Even the way de Haan was killed," Jason interrupted. He couldn't help circling back to the thing preying on him the most. "That crime scene."

"Go on."

"He was fully dressed, lying face up on the made bed. It looked like he'd been hit from behind. There was significant head trauma, but the blood was all—or at least mostly—on de Haan's clothes. If he'd been attacked in that room, there was nothing to show for it. No blood spray, no overturned furniture, no soaked sheets… His laptop was there, his phone was there. No attempt had been made to hide him or set the scene to look like a robbery or anything else. I just don't understand."

"And you're not likely to get a copy of the forensics report from Sandford."

"Hell no." Jason took another bite of salad, swallowed, said bleakly, "JDLR."

Sam grimaced at the copspeak for Just Doesn't Look Right.

"De Haan is a stranger in town. Hell, he's a stranger in the country. What is the motive for murdering him?"

Sam said, "It sounds like you have a theory."

"I wish. But if it's a random attack, how does that happen? If it didn't happen in his motel room, and it sure didn't look like it to me—"

"You can't know without seeing the forensics report."

"Okay, fair enough, appearances can be deceiving, and it's just supposition so far, but if he wasn't killed in that room, if it was a random attack, why on earth would his murderer take him back to his motel room?"

"Possible theories?"

Jason grimaced. "He was killed in a mugging, and Police Chief Sandford had his body returned to his motel room so as not to upset the tourist trade."

Sam snorted. "You don't believe that."

"Hell no, I don't believe that. It has to do with van Apeldoorn v. Thompson. But then...like I said, there really isn't any motive for murder." He thought it over. "Except..."

"Except?"

"De Haan was convinced the Thompsons are concealing the rest of the items taken from Engelshofen Castle. What if he went looking for them?"

"Let's say he did. Let's say he even found something. It's quite a jump from lying about looted art to committing murder."

"I know. But those missing pieces are worth a lot of money. That Vermeer alone—"

"Even so. You're talking about two very different psychological profiles."

"But that kind of crossover happens. *Shadow on the Glass*—your own book—details a couple of cases where petty criminals escalate to violent, horrific crimes."

"There's a sexual component in all those cases that's missing here. Your subjects are not the perpetrators of the original theft. They had zero involvement. At most, they're guilty of concealing evidence, lying to federal investigators, and hiding stolen property. Correct?"

"Well, yes. But—"

"The murder of de Haan is a very different skill set, and—as you pointed out yourself—no principal in your case has a strong motive for eliminating your victim."

"Crazy isn't enough of a motive?"

"In my discipline, yes. In yours, no."

"Hm. Well, I don't know about that lack of motive theory," Jason said. "If de Haan was correct and the Thompson family is hiding the rest of the treasure, I think several million dollars is a pretty decent motive."

Sam's pale brows rose. "Several *million*?"

"Yes. If the Vermeer *is* part of that treasure trove, it's probably worth at least ten million. In fact, given the legendary status of the painting, I think it would be worth a lot more."

"But this particular Vermeer is a myth, isn't it?"

"No. Well, yes. The painting did exist at one time, but it could well be history now. Literally. But there was some painting in that treasure trove that fits the general description, which is pretty unique in paintings by Dutch Masters. Or anyone else."

"How so?"

"Interior. In which a gentleman is washing his hands in a perspectival room with figures, artful and rare."

"That's the title?"

"Title and description."

"And that's a rare scene in Dutch art?"

"It is, yes. At least as far as gentlemen go. There's a fair bit of ladies washing their hands. But really, there's not a whole lot of handwashing in Vermeer of either sex. There's some foot washing and some jug pouring, but no handwashing. The washing of hands was probably an allegory for cleansing the soul, but that just makes it all the more interesting."

Sam made a you-don't-say expression and took a swallow of his drink.

"I'm guessing he probably used the composition of *Girl Reading a Letter at an Open Window*. He liked that window a lot. At first, I was thinking he might have used the same composition as in *The Milkmaid* or *Young Woman with a Water Pitcher*, but the addition of the 'artful and rare figures' would require a more elegant setting."

"Sure," Sam said in the tone of one humoring a difficult patient.

"Sorry. I'm babbling." Jason rubbed his forehead. He really did want to believe in that Vermeer. And he really was *very* tired.

"Hey," Sam said softly. Jason's eyes flashed up to meet his gaze. "You're not babbling. A little overstimulated maybe, but you're making perfect sense to me. And I'm not saying you're wrong about the motive behind de Haan's murder. The Thompsons may not be a good fit, but a random act of violence seems even less likely."

Jason's smile was wry. "Thanks."

"You want to get out of here?"

"Yeah, I do."

On the drive back to their hotel, it occurred to Jason it might be very useful—even invaluable—to get Sam's perspective on Captain Roy Thompson. Not so much as it related to his current and ongoing investigation, but for getting a reading on Thompson and his original crime. Even if Sam only did a cursory, off-the-cuff psychological profile on Thompson, it would give Jason better insight on what type of offender he was investigating. Specifically, how likely it was that Captain Thompson had acted alone or on his own recognizance, how prone his personality type might be to lying, the types of lies he might tell, what might motivate him to implicate an innocent party in his crime…

But not only did Sam have his own crushing workload—partly self-inflicted, but still—there was a high probability he was going to notice what no one else had so far: Jason's personal connection to the case.

Okay, what if he did notice? It would be a relief at this point to be able to share his concerns. Even when they disagreed, there was no one whose opinion Jason trusted or whose judgment he valued more than Sam's.

He continued to weigh the pros and cons as they walked into the hotel lobby.

Sam glanced at the elevators, said, "Your place or mine?"

"Yours," Jason replied. "I've got Russell in the room next to me."

The elevator doors opened, and Sam put his hand on the small of Jason's back to usher him in. Jason stepped back and said, "Can I ask a favor?"

Sam's brows rose. "Of course."

"Will you look over the original case notes regarding Roy Thompson? I mean de Haan's research as well as my own."

"Of course." Sam did a double take. "You mean *now*?"

"I know. It's a lot to ask."

Sam's smile was crooked. "Not so much. Get the file, West. Let's have a look."

Jason brought the file up to Sam's room. Sam, by then in jeans and shirtsleeves, had ordered room service from the bar and was pouring a drink. He held up the bottle of Canadian Club. Jason shook his head and handed him the folder.

Sam sat down at the desk, half turning his chair so that he could prop his feet on the end of the bed. He put his glasses on and began to read.

Jason sat on the foot of the bed to wait.

The blood-red sunset faded to twilight and deepened to dusk. The stars came out.

Jason walked out onto the balcony, watched for lucky stars for a while, failed to find any, and came back in. He circled the room.

Without looking up from the file, Sam said, "The pacing is distracting."

"Right. Sorry." Jason sat on the foot of the bed, smothered a yawn with both hands.

Sam sighed, raised his head. "Go to bed, West. I'll join you as soon as I finish."

Jason blinked owlishly at him. "You sure?"

Sam's wry grin was answer enough.

"Okay. If I don't wake up, nudge me." He undressed down to his boxers, pulled the comforter back, and climbed between the sheets. He was pretty sure he was too wound up to sleep, but the idea of resting his eyes sounded like heaven.

Sam said absently, "Sleep well."

The next time Jason opened his eyes, the sun was coming up. The room was misty with rose-gold light, and the quiet was bliss. Too early for maid service, too early for downtown traffic, and even the air conditioner was silent. He glanced over at the other side of the mattress.

No Sam.

He raised his head, blinking, and saw that Sam was still sitting at the desk, gazing out the window. The file folder was lying closed on the desk. His glasses were folded on top.

At Jason's movement, Sam glanced at him.

He said in a quiet voice Jason had never heard before, "How is it you got permission to work this case?"

Jason sat up. He said cautiously, "What do you mean? De Haan approached me."

"You know what I mean. MFAA Deputy Chief Emerson Harley is your grandfather."

"Yes." Okay, he had known Sam would probably recognize his grandfather's name. And he had figured Sam would disapprove of his decision to work the case rather than recuse himself. He had also figured that Sam would recognize his efforts to stay objective—it was right there in his written analysis for Sam to read. He wasn't concealing, covering, condoning. He was simply gathering the facts—all the facts. He had assured himself it would be okay, but there was a note in Sam's voice that seemed to catch him mid-heartbeat.

Sam said in that deadly quiet voice, "You've got a conflict of interest as wide as the Danube. How did you convince Kapszukiewicz to grant an individual waiver in this case?"

Despite the sudden dryness of his mouth, Jason said steadily, "I didn't. I didn't disclose my potential conflict of interest."

"You didn't tell Kapszukiewicz and you didn't consult an ethics official?" The lack of any...*anything* in Sam's voice was far more alarming than if he'd raised his voice. "Did you discuss this with your squad supervisor, your SAC or your ADC?"

"No." Jason rushed on to say, "Because there *isn't* a conflict, Sam. Not really. I know my grandfather was not involved. He did not give Thompson those items or even permission to move them to a safer local."

Sam started to speak. Jason kept talking, "I know what you're going to say, but I have the advantage of having known the man. But that's beside the point. I'm investigating this as I would any other case. You've got both my notes and de Haan's in front of you. You can see I'm not trying to lead the inquiry in any direction; I'm not trying to conceal anything. It's all there. I'm following the trail to wherever it leads. If that wasn't the truth, I wouldn't have asked you to look at the files."

Granted, if he hadn't been a little smashed and so tired he couldn't see straight, he wouldn't have asked Sam to look at the files. He could see now that had been a huge tactical error.

Sam put on his glasses, picked up his phone, and read aloud, "*5 C.F. R. Section 2635.501 through 503 (Subpart E - Impartiality in Performing Official Duties). In addition to the impartiality regulation, 28 C.F.R. Section 45.2 prohibits a DOJ employee, without written authorization, from participating in a criminal investigation or prosecution if he has a personal or political relationship with any person or organization substantially involved in the conduct that is the subject of the investigation or prosecution, or any person or organization which he knows has a specific and substantial interest that would be directly affected by the outcome of the investigation or prosecution.*

"Tell me what part of that you don't understand."

Jason said stiffly, "I understand every part of that."

"Tell me which part of that is news to you."

"No part of that section of the Code of Federal Regulations is news to me."

"Tell me the part you think doesn't apply to you."

Jason controlled his temper. "I know it all applies to me."

Sam stared at him for a long moment. "Then what the fuck do you think you're doing, West?"

In this context, "West" was not remotely a pet name.

"I think I'm working a case I am best qualified to investigate."

Sam put a hand to his temple as though he thought his head was about to split open. He said in that same tight, terse tone, "You don't get to make that call."

Jason opened his mouth, but Sam overrode him.

"And if you think this isn't a real problem, let's phone Kapszukiewicz right now. Let's explain the situation to her and see what she has to say."

Jason closed his mouth.

Sam's smile was humorless. "That's what I thought. You've not only compromised yourself and your investigation, you've compromised me."

Jason felt the blood drain from his face.

"Was it your expectation that I would keep this information to myself, or did you assume I'd contact your superiors?"

Jason said nothing. He was genuinely stricken.

Into his shattered silence, Sam said, "So you're making me complicit in this clusterfuck."

"That was…not my intent."

"Good to know." Sam's eyes looked like ice chips.

Jason sucked in a sharp breath, said, "Call Kapszukiewicz, then. Go ahead. Tell her everything. I don't care. But I didn't— It was not my— If you believe I'm morally, ethically, fundamentally compromised, then whatever. I'm not asking you to cover for me."

Sam rose. Jason rose as well, ready for...well, Jesus, were they going to punch it out? He had no idea. He had never seen Sam this angry, had never imagined that level of anger could be directed at himself. In a faraway corner of his brain, he wondered if he was dreaming.

*This can't be happening.*

But they did not come to blows. They did not get within touching distance.

Sam said in that strangely flat voice, "Take your file and get out of my room," and then went into the bathroom.

Jason stood unmoving; then he dressed with shaking hands, grabbed the folder, and left Sam's hotel room.

# CHAPTER FOURTEEN

"**W**hat if de Haan spotted a Nazi war criminal living in Bozwin?" J.J. asked.

"Hm?"

It was about ten o'clock on Thursday morning, and Jason and J.J. were in their temporary office at the Bozwin RA. J.J. was bringing Jason up to date on the results of his inquiries the day before.

"That's a pretty powerful motive. And it's possible when you see how many of these old geezers are still hanging out at the VFW."

Jason nodded. He was scrolling quickly through his email, looking for something, anything, from Karan or George or even Sam.

There was nothing.

He was not sure if he was relieved or not. He had no idea what Sam would do next—if anything. He was still shell-shocked from Sam's reaction earlier that morning. He had known Sam would not be pleased, yes, had expected Sam to advise him to recuse himself at once. He had not expected… *that*.

And maybe it was naive, but he felt betrayed. If anyone ought to understand about shades of gray, he'd have figured it was BAU Chief Sam Kennedy. Also, if anyone ought to understand about occasionally ignoring protocol, you'd think it was that same asshole, BAU Chief Sam Kennedy. For God's sake. How about Wyoming? How about New York? How about Massachusetts? How about was there *any* fucking place on the planet Sam had not flouted rules and regulations when he felt he could get faster and better results by doing so?

And yet, maybe Jason should have expected it, because despite his tendency to operate in a legal twilight when it seemed imperative to him, Sam could be very black and white about other people bending rules. And once you got on his bad side? Well, it wasn't that Sam was vengeful or spiteful. Not remotely. You were just dead to him.

In fairness, Sam had worked hard to position himself where it was difficult for his enemies—and he had his share—to attack him. Jason had inadvertently endangered that unassailable position, and therefore, Sam's mission, and Sam had a sense of mission like no one Jason had ever known.

No, scratch that. The only other person Jason had known with such a sense of mission was his grandfather. Now there was irony.

J.J. said, "Are you still planning to reinterview Roberts?"

At the same time, Sam was pragmatic, a realist about people. Wasn't there a decent chance that once he'd cooled down enough to view the situation objectively, he would see that Jason had not intended to make him complicit in any wrongdoing?

*The road to hell is paved with good intentions, West.* He could almost hear Sam whispering it in his ear.

"West?"

Jason looked up. "What's that?"

"Are you going to have another try at Edgar Roberts?"

"Yes."

"Because I can take him if you want—"

"No. I'll talk to him. I need you to get what information you can about de Haan's murder from Sandford's office. No way is anyone over there going to talk to me now."

"Right." J.J.'s gaze was curious. "It is weird Sandford didn't want to question you."

"It sure as hell is. He couldn't get rid of me fast enough. Almost for good."

J.J. made a pained expression. He had been skeptical when Jason had told him he believed Sandford had considered shooting him the previous day.

"You don't believe me," Jason said. "But something was going on there, and I don't think it's only that he doesn't like Uncle Sam traipsing through his backyard and throwing our weight around. Maybe he's in Thompson's will."

"Maybe he's worried about us discovering his Nazi grandfather."

"Huh?"

"Never mind. I don't remember seeing any bequests to Sandford in the will. I'll take another look. Are you headed back to the newspaper morgue?"

Jason nodded, shrugging into his suit jacket. He picked up the rental's keys.

J.J. started to turn to his laptop and then stopped. "Oh. I finally spoke to Larry Johnson."

"Who?"

"Quilletta's first husband."

"The Winter Squash King?"

J.J. grinned. "No. That was husband number two. Larry is the one who ran off with his high-school sweetheart. He's living in Arizona now."

"What does he have to say for himself?"

"He thinks his daughter is married to a dangerous felon and we should do something about that."

Jason shook his head in resignation. "I wonder what it is he thinks we can do."

"And he says he does not remember Roy ever showing any treasures of any kind to anyone. Particularly him."

"Great."

"I think he's lying. He sounded like someone who had been practicing in front of a mirror."

"Why would he lie to protect his ex-wife?"

"Maybe he still loves her. Who knows? He didn't have anything bad to say about her. For what it's worth."

It was disappointing. Jason had been hoping one of the ex-husbands would provide a chink in the wall of solidarity the Thompsons' friends and neighbors had put up around them. So far, they had been unable to find anyone who would admit to Roy Thompson showing them anything that remotely fit the description of treasure.

"Maybe there *was* an accomplice," J.J. said. "Maybe the accomplice got the lion's share of the treasure."

"Maybe. Don't forget to call Bozwin PD and see what they'll give you on de Haan's homicide."

J.J. looked heavenward. "What would I do without you telling me how to do my job, West?"

"I'll tell you when I think of it." Jason winked and closed the door to the office.

\* \* \* \* \*

*Yesterday I was left alone and went down to the tunnels, which remain our art-collection depot. I spent the whole day looking at really amazing pictures. They are stacked up like books against the wall, and the frames are often heavy, but the glories are undiminished. Painting is so wonderful. Few people can know the rewards of such glorious workmanship and heavenly color. We are doing important work here, and I am proud to be part of it.*

Jason's heart jumped and skipped its way down every line of the letter dated July 1945 and published two months later in the *Bozwin Daily Chronicle*.

There was no mention of Emerson Harley by name. Thank God for small mercies. Not that it would be impossible for someone to find out which member of the MFAA had been stationed at Engelshofen Castle.

His phone rang, and Karan Kapszukiewicz's name flashed up.

Jason's heart dropped through the trapdoor of his stomach. He waited for a moment, watching the little speaker emblem pulse. What was the point of putting this off? He was out of time. He pressed Accept.

"Ma'am."

"Jason," Karan said. "Any update on the de Haan homicide?"

She sounded her normal crisp but cordial self. Jason responded cautiously, "Nothing so far. J.J. is following up with Bozwin PD. I should tell you the police chief is pretty unhappy with our presence on his turf."

"Is that Amos Sandford?"

"Yes."

"I've got a stack of messages on my desk from him."

"I bet."

"Well, if he doesn't like us nosing around, he'd better hurry up and solve our complainant's homicide." She paused. "Look, Jason." Karan's tone changed, and he braced for the worst. "I understand there's some concern over the wrongful-death suit filed by the parents of the young man killed in Monday's shootout."

With everything else going on, Jason had practically forgotten about the lawsuit filed by Brody Stevens's family.

"Yes," he said automatically.

"This is not official. You did not hear it from me. However, I have it on good authority that the SIRG is going to deem the use of lethal force demonstrated by both you and Agent Russell justified."

"That's…a relief."

It was. But he had never doubted it. By now he had been over the shooting dozens of times in his mind, and he still did not see that he and J.J. had had any other choice. He felt horrible about the Stevens kid, but he would have felt worse if they'd let him shoot an innocent bystander.

"You know how this works, so maybe you can explain it to your partner. If this does go to trial, you'll be represented by the DOJ. There is no cause for panic, so could you please tell

Agent Russell to stop phoning and emailing everyone in his company address book?"

Jason winced. "Yes, I'll do that."

"Thank you." She hesitated. "Getting cleared by the SIRG is one thing. If Russell is having trouble coming to terms with his actions, you could remind him that counseling is available. In fact, whether he's having trouble or not, that would be my recommendation if he were on my team."

"I've suggested it to him."

"I see. If you have concerns, you should broach them with George Potts. You're relying on Russell to watch your back. That's not something you want to make a mistake about."

"No. Right. I understand."

She said briskly, getting ready to end the call, "Right. Anything new to report?"

Sam had not told her. Jason absorbed the truth with a feeling of disbelief. And yet...had he really thought Sam *would*?

"No," he said slowly. "Nothing new yet."

"All right. Keep me apprised."

Karan rang off. Jason stared at his phone, then returned to the archives.

Two hours later, in a letter dated September 1945, he finally found what he had been looking for—and dreading.

*For the last few weeks since Deputy Chief Harley left, there has been nothing but tedious work and horrible Germans. There is absolutely no one to talk to this gloomy intellectual misfit.*

So that was that. Thompson didn't have to come right out and say Emerson Harley had acted as his accomplice. Others would make that connection.

If they found this.

For one terrible, heart-thudding moment he considered ripping out the page.

But no. It was not in him to destroy a historical document. Not even an old newspaper. Hell, it was not even in him to hide it. The fact that the idea had even crossed his mind was shocking enough.

Besides, what good would it do? At best, he could delay the discovery that his grandfather had been the officer in charge of the art-collection depot while Thompson was there.

The truth will out.

That was both the good news and the bad.

Truth was also supposed to set you free, so something to look forward to, right?

If he did truly believe his grandfather was innocent—and he did—why would he try to suppress the facts?

For the first time since he had spotted Emerson Harley's name in de Haan's report, Jason asked himself what his grandfather would have wanted. What would he have done in Jason's position?

And the answer was so obvious, it felt like a slap upside the head—something Jason's grandfather had never delivered in real life.

Emerson Harley had never ducked a fight in his life. He would have challenged any and all allegations directly, dragging them out into the light and knocking them down, one by one. And if he knew the moral compromises Jason was making to "defend" his honor, he'd have been appalled.

*I don't need you to defend my good name. My good name* is *my defense.* That's what Emerson Harley would have said.

And he'd have been right.

His cell phone rang, the moment of epiphany ended like a burst bubble, and Jason answered automatically.

J.J. said, "To start with, it turns out I was right. Thompson was gay. I told you so."

"Uh, yes. You did."

"But that's not why he couldn't get his old teaching job back after the war. Nobody knew about it back then."

"Why couldn't he get his job back?" Jason asked.

"Because he'd received a dishonorable discharge in December 1945. He was court-martialed and fined $600 for the theft of valuable silverware and gold-decorated china from the villa of the Marquise of St. Carlos in Biarritz, France."

"You're kidding."

"Nope."

"That's good work. Yours, I mean."

"I thought so," J.J. said with his usual modesty. "What do you think the family is trying to hide? The fact that he was gay, or the fact that he was a known thief?"

"Both? I'm not sure. I'm not sure those are the only things they're trying to hide."

"Well, the treasures, of course, but it looks like Thompson had less time to steal things from Engelshofen Castle than we realized."

"Yes." And more time to steal things elsewhere.

"Maybe it *was* just the two paintings and the altar piece. I sure can't come up with anyone who admits to seeing any of the other items."

"Did you find someone who had seen the two paintings and the altar piece?"

"No."

"Then I'd say that doesn't prove anything." Jason considered. "Who do we have left to talk to?"

"Nobody."

"What about the first husband?"

"We had this conversation this morning, West. He said he never saw any treasures."

*Had* they discussed this? Jesus.

"Right. How long were they married?"

"Three years. What does that have to do with it?"

Pretty much nothing. At this point Jason was just bumping into walls. Detective Roomba looking for an opening, any opening.

"What about the second husband?"

J.J. sighed. Pointedly. "He split up with the girlfriend. I haven't been able to locate him yet."

Had they had this conversation too?

"Did you actually talk to the girlfriend?"

"Hell yes, I talked to the girlfriend. She's suing him for eight years of back child support. You know, this is not my first investigation."

"I know. Sorry. I'm just...distracted."

"I noticed. You should try getting some sleep once in a while. When are you coming back to the office?"

Jason thought about all those binders of all those newspapers. What was it he imagined was still left to find? A public declaration that MFAA Deputy Chief Emerson Harley had not taken part in the theft of national treasures under his protection?

He was not going to find that magic seal of approval.

And the truth was, he didn't need it. He never had.

He said, "Now."

# CHAPTER FIFTEEN

"**S**o here's what we know," J.J. said. "De Haan was not killed in his room. He was killed at an unknown location and his body dumped in his motel room."

"*Why?*" Jason said. "That's the second question. Why was no effort made to hide the body?"

J.J. glanced at the clock over the empty bookcase. "Okay. What's the first question?"

"Why was he killed at all?"

J.J. shook his head. "What's the answer?"

"To the second question? They didn't want us looking for him. They didn't want us poking around, getting search warrants—"

"They?" J.J. asked cautiously.

"They."

J.J. clearly decided to let that go. He moved on through his notes. "Estimated time of death *maybe* around midnight. The temperature of the room complicates things. Cause of death: blunt force trauma to the back of the skull. Weapon unknown, but something heavy and smooth, and edged. An iron? Not a brick. Not a rock. Here's something interesting. Factory reset was used to delete everything on his phone."

"The data can still be retrieved. His phone records can still be accessed."

"In theory, yes. But who's going to do that? Not Bozwin PD, I'll tell you right now."

"What are they calling it?"

"Robbery homicide."

"That makes *no* sense. Was he even robbed?"

"According to…" J.J. looked at his notes. "Detective Wallace, yes. De Haan's wallet and passport are missing." J.J. glanced again at the clock. He said wearily, "Look, West, I know you think there's something hinky going on, but it's not our case."

"It's part of our case. I guarantee it."

"Yeah, well, I'm not even sure *our* case is still our case. We've been trying for three days to find someone, *anyone*, who can verify Roy Thompson ever had more than that altar piece and those two paintings in his possession. Even if you're right, even if de Haan was right, how do we move forward without proof?"

"I'm telling you, they killed him. And I want to know why."

"*They* again. You mean the Thompsons? *All* of them?"

"The Thompsons and Sandford."

"Okay, wait. Now it's the Thompsons *and* Sandford?" J.J. shook his head. "No offense, but you're starting to sound a little…"

He didn't bother to fill in the blank.

Jason said, "Just…look at it objectively for a moment. I mean, come on. De Haan is randomly killed by some stranger who conveniently returns his body to his motel room? Who the hell does that?"

"Okay, fine, but why the hell would the Thompsons and Sandford do that? It doesn't make any sense from that perspective either." J.J. added, "And people—even private investigators from other countries—do get randomly killed. It doesn't always make sense."

Jason snapped, "It's too much of a coincidence!"

J.J. shot back, "We're not cops!"

They glared at each other. Jason raked a hand through his hair, sighed. "I know. I realize that. But you know as well as I do that this stinks to high heaven."

"Okay," J.J. said. "Maybe I agree that this whole thing looks fishy as shit. *You're* the one who said there was no motive for the Thompsons to get rid of de Haan. Even if they do have the rest of the treasure, it would be a lot easier just to make a deal with the various entities than commit murder and then *still* not be able to move those items for God knows how long. Maybe forever. It's not like a Vermeer can just pop up and no one is going to notice. And if even *one* of those items shows up, it's tantamount to confessing they've got everything. In fact, according to your latest theory, it would be tantamount to confessing murder. *Why* would they do that? It makes *no* sense."

"I know it makes no sense, but that's what happened. I *know* it is."

J.J. was shaking his head. "And why would Sandford go along with this?"

"He's a friend of the family."

"I'll say. If he's willing to help them commit murder."

"From the minute we arrived, Sandford wanted to go to war. Why?"

"He doesn't like feebs. Are you pretending you've never bumped into a cop with an attitude before?"

"I think it's more than that. Why did Bert Thompson call Sandford when we showed up at his ranch?"

"You just said it. He's a friend of the family."

"I've been thinking a lot about this. Sandford arrived before anyone else, including the Park County Sheriffs. It took us nearly an hour to drive out to the ranch. How did he get there so fast? I think Thompson called him *before* the shooting. I think he was already on his way."

J.J. opened his mouth, closed it.

"Something else," Jason said. "When I first contacted Sandford's office to let them know we'd be interviewing people locally, he refused to take my calls or answer my emails."

"We're going in circles. He doesn't like feebs. He's not alone in that. It doesn't prove anything."

"Not on its own, but when you put it all together—"

J.J. groaned. "When you put it all together, it sounds like the conspiracy theory of a guy who hasn't had much sleep in the last month. That's what it sounds like to me." He closed his laptop and got to his feet. "I don't know about you, but I've got dinner plans tonight. If you want to tackle this again tomorrow when we're both fresh, okay. Apparently, we're not ever going home, so yeah, let's hash it out tomorrow when we've both—hopefully—had some sleep."

"I got plenty of sleep last night," Jason said shortly.

"Really? 'Coz Kennedy looks trashed today."

Jason was silent.

J.J. grabbed his jacket. "I'm getting a ride with Martinez, so the car's yours tonight."

Jason nodded.

J.J. hesitated at the door. "Seriously, West, you need a night off."

Jason nodded again. "Thanks. I'll talk to you tomorrow."

J.J. went out, closing the door.

Jason sighed, scrubbed his face with both hands. He *was* tired, but that didn't mean he was wrong about this. De Haan's death was not random, not accidental. It was directly related to this case. And no, it didn't make sense. Because they didn't have all the facts yet. Once they did, those facts would show the Thompsons and Police Chief Sandford were in this thing up to their collective necks.

But how the hell was he supposed to gather those facts? He had no idea.

J.J. was right about one thing: sitting here as the daylight leeched away was not getting him anywhere.

He rose, grabbed his things, left the office—and was in time to see Travis Petty step out of Sam's office.

"Exactly," Petty said. He was laughing as he closed Sam's door. He glanced over, spotted Jason, and his expression instantly closed down.

Jason felt a surge of ridiculous and confused emotion. Jealousy, hurt, irritation.

Petty nodded, passing Jason. There was a hint of curiosity in his blue gaze. Jason nodded in return, waiting until Petty went into his office.

Jason glanced at Sam's closed door.

Weird the difference twenty-four hours could make. Yesterday at this time… Well, probably better not to dwell on yesterday. Not if he was going to get through today with his dignity intact.

At the same time, it felt crazy, impossible, that he couldn't just go *talk* to Sam.

For God's sake, they had been talking nonstop for almost a year.

As angry as Sam had been this morning, he couldn't *want* this situation any more than Jason did.

It wasn't possible to instantly stop loving someone.

Or at least it wasn't possible for Jason.

Sam… Well, as much as Jason loved Sam, Sam had his quirks. No question.

He continued to linger in the hall, trying to make up his mind. In the end, he walked down to Sam's office because it was almost physically impossible for him not to do so. Despite his reluctance to face the Sam of that morning, the connection he felt was simply too strong to ignore.

He knocked softly on the door.

"Come." Sam's voice was crisp.

Jason opened the door.

Sam looked up.

He did not seem surprised to see Jason. He did not seem much of anything. There was no smile, no welcome in his eyes.

It was painful for Jason to realize how much he had come to take for granted—to rely on—the welcome in Sam's eyes.

"Can we talk?"

Sam's head bent in silent, unsmiling assent.

Okay, J.J. had been right about two things. Sam did look haggard. There were lines in his face that hadn't been there yesterday and shadows beneath his eyes.

Jason closed the door and leaned against it. He did not want anyone walking in on this conversation; also, he did not miss the fact that he was not being invited to sit.

"It...hurts that you think I would try to bury the truth or—or manipulate the facts to suit myself or my family. I wouldn't do that. I would *never* do that."

Sam said—and he sounded tired, "People find good reasons for doing the wrong things. You're not the first. You won't be the last."

"I wanted to know the truth. That's all. And I felt like I was the best person to discover what that is because I *am* biased."

Sam's mouth curved, but it was not a friendly smile.

Jason pushed on. That's what it felt like: trying to push a boulder up a hill. "I know how this looks on the surface, but I also know the kind of man my grandfather was. He dedicated his life to the preservation of art. He was willing to risk his life. He didn't have to go overseas. He wasn't drafted. He was forty-six and a lieutenant in the Navy Reserve. He *requested* active duty, but because of his art-conservation background, he agreed to join the newly formed Monuments, Fine Arts, and Archives program."

Sam said, "I know all this. I know how much you admired and loved your grandfather. I know that his work with the Monuments Men inspired your own decision to dedicate your life to the protection and preservation of art. I understand—

more than you realize—that this is not easy for you, which is why you needed to hand if off to an agent who did not have a personal stake in the outcome."

Jason started to speak, but Sam cut across. "Do you not understand that because you are ethically compromised, your investigation is compromised? Even if you do find that your grandfather had no involvement whatsoever in the theft of these items, your personal bias makes your findings dubious at best."

"I know that's a risk, but—"

"It's not a risk. It's a fact."

"Which is why it was my intention to find irrefutable proof that my grandfather was not involved."

"Okay, and do you understand that comment is not remotely reassuring?"

"You know what I mean."

"You know what I know? Your good intentions are irrelevant. What *is* relevant is you've knowingly, deliberately, violated ethics regulations. You're throwing your career away—and for what?"

Jason was silent. He had hoped that with a bit of time to cool down and process, Sam's hard-line view of the situation might soften. But if anything, his perspective had solidified, hardened. He was no longer angry. This cold conviction was worse than that.

He said finally, bitterly, "I see. So where does that leave us?"

Sam did not answer.

Jason said, "Would you like your ring back?"

That was pure sarcasm, because of course Sam had not given him a ring. They had never so much as discussed rings—or even the future. Not in any real or practical way.

Sam's eyes grew grayer, flintier. He said, "Do you think this is easy for me?"

"No. But I don't think I realized how difficult it was going to be."

He was trying to be fair about this. He understood why Sam was upset. Understood that he had inadvertently placed Sam in an awkward position. But wouldn't it have been worse to continue to conceal the truth? He understood that Sam disapproved of his choices up and down the line. Understood that while Sam was capable of violating protocol when he deemed it necessary, he took a seriously dim view of anyone else doing so.

Sam said, "No? Well, finding out the person you love can't be trusted is a big fucking deal in my book."

Jason forgot about trying to be fair or trying to see things from Sam's point of view.

"Can't be *trusted*?" His voice shook, but that was plain old fury, nothing more. "I can be trusted in every way that counts. And if you don't know that—"

Sam's voice rose—and he rose with it. Towering over the desk. "*You* don't get to decide what ways count for me. You *lied*—"

"I didn't lie. I withheld information. Which you have also done in the past."

Sam snapped, "I withheld information when you were injured, and I did so on the advice and with the approval of your doctor."

Okay, well, Jason hadn't realized Sam had bothered to check with his doctors regarding how much to tell him after he'd been injured. Maybe he should have. Even so.

There were surely plenty of other instances of Sam's high-handed behavior, but in the heat of the moment they escaped him. Or maybe there were just too many to choose from.

"Are you seriously going to pretend that if you thought keeping me in the dark was in my best interests, you wouldn't have overruled that advice?"

Sam said flatly, "I would not do anything that could potentially compromise you either physically or professionally."

That was the simple, unvarnished truth. Jason had to acknowledge it.

"Fair enough." He met Sam's gaze steadily. "Again, I did not mean to compromise you. I'm sorry. I've apologized, and if I could undo it, I would. I don't know what more I can say or do." It was not easy to ask, but he had to know. "Are we— Are you— Is it over between us? Is that what you want?"

"Of course it's not what I want. I love you. But." It was Sam's turn to take a deep breath. For a moment, his face looked harrowed. Clearly, this was not easy for him either. Clearly, he was in pain. Knowing that only made it worse. "I feel that I don't know you. The person I thought you were would not have done this."

Probably would have hurt less if Sam had simply kicked him in the face. As it was, it was all Jason could do to manage an even, "I see."

To which Sam said nothing.

*Nothing.*

Not because he was being deliberately cruel, but because that was how he felt. He had told Jason the truth and, it seemed, did not have anything else to add.

And as hard as Jason was trying to be fair and look at it from Sam's point of view, he was simply in too much pain to take it without fighting back.

"Well, if you decide we're no longer whatever the hell it is we're supposed to be, can you at least tell me to my face this time? I don't want a phone call or a text or an email."

Sam didn't like that. His eyes narrowed. His mouth thinned.

"Anything I have to say to you, West, I'll tell you in person."

"Can't wait," Jason returned. "In the meantime?"

Sam didn't even hesitate. "I think we both need time apart."

Jason nodded, opened the office door, stepped out, and closed it quietly behind him.

# CHAPTER SIXTEEN

*C*an't be trusted.

Jason slammed out through the glass doors of the Bozwin RA and stalked toward the parking lot. Any tears at that point would have been tears of rage, but there were no tears in him. His eyes were dry and burning. His heart felt like something spewed out of a volcano, red-hot and pulsing.

He was hurt and angry—more angry than hurt for now, which made the immediate future easier—and yes, he knew he was largely to blame for his problems. But not entirely. For Sam Kennedy, the keeper of secrets, to tell Jason *he* couldn't be trusted?

Jesus fucking Christ.

Talk about being blind to your own faults. Talk about the pot calling the kettle black. Talk about... Well, no need to worry about talking because he would die before he ever voluntarily said another word to that goddamned arrogant asshole—

"Agent West?" someone called.

Jason spun—and he half hoped it *would* be Jeremy Kyser on the other end of that high, strained voice because he dearly wanted to strangle someone with his bare hands.

But no. Baby Mayhew stood on the curb next to the No Parking zone.

"Yes?"

His expression must have been pretty alarming because she clutched her purse in front of her with both hands like a little old lady afraid of being mugged.

"You said I could speak to you at any time…"

He had to take a couple of steadying breaths. He was still so furious, he was shaking.

*Can't be trusted.*

He had spent his entire adult life being the guy *everyone* trusted. Reliable. Responsible. Reasonable.

You know who couldn't be trusted? Goddamned Sam Kennedy, who made the rules up as he went along. Who believed rules were for other people. Who turned his emotions on and off like he was flicking a freaking switch.

He realized Baby's big brown eyes were still fixed on him as she waited for his response.

"Yes," he said, and he was surprised his voice sounded so normal. "Did you want to come inside and make a statement?"

"Oh no." She looked alarmed at the very idea. "No, I just wanted to give you this." She unsnapped her purse, reached in, and he braced for… Well, given the day he was having, getting shot would not have come as a total surprise. It might even be a relief.

She drew out something that shone and sparkled in the fading sunlight.

A gold locket.

He blinked at it as it swung gently from her hand, twisting and turning like a stage magician's magical amulet.

"My great-uncle gave this to me when I turned sixteen."

Even if Jason hadn't seen the black and white photos, he would have recognized the locket from its description.

*Circa 1920. Heart-shaped locket exquisitely detailed in 14kt yellow gold with 9 .12 ct. diamonds, suspended from pleated gold chain.*

He reached for it, and she slipped the chain from her fingers and let him take it. He stared at the fragile chain threaded through his fingers. Somehow it had survived all these years. That had to be a metaphor for something, but he was too tired and heartsick to think what.

"Were there photos inside?"

Her lips trembled. She nodded. "Two. Old sepia pictures of a man and a little girl."

"Do you still have the photos?"

Baby shook her head. "I was a kid. It never occurred to me— *I* didn't want them. I wanted my own photos—so I took them out and threw them away."

Someone else's heartbreak. But the Rosensteins would probably remind him they had lost a lot more than photos.

Baby said, "Uncle Roy was like that. Generous. He gave things away to the people he liked. I thought—we all thought—they were his to give."

"Yes." Jason did believe that.

"But now that I know…"

"Did your great-uncle give you other things?"

"No. Well, the five thousand dollars in his will. But nothing else. Nothing like *that*." She nodded at the locket. Jason found that he believed her.

"Why are you bringing this to me now?"

Her throat jerked as she swallowed. "You were...nice yesterday. Kind. About the...not lying. And the things you said made me think." She looked apologetic. "Gary doesn't trust the police. He got into trouble a long time ago, and he thinks the police are always trying to get people. To trick them. But it seemed to me you were saying if you could get those pictures and the other things back, you didn't really *care* about anything else."

Jason said, "Where you're concerned, no. I don't care about anything else. You were a kid when your uncle gave you this locket. And as far as Gary, I don't have anything against him. So long as he stays out of my case, I don't see that changing."

"Gary's not involved."

Did she have any idea how revealing that statement was? No. She did not.

Jason said, "Can I ask you something? You say your great-uncle was generous. Why was Bert's daughter, your cousin Patty, left out of the will?"

Baby bit her lip. "Uncle Roy was funny about Cindy and Patty. He didn't approve of my Uncle Bert's lifestyle."

"*He* didn't approve of *Bert's* lifestyle?"

"When my Uncle Bert was younger, he was kind of wild. He used to hang out in bars a lot and get into fights. But then he met Cindy, and everything changed. Except Uncle Roy didn't want him to marry my aunt Cindy. For one thing, Cindy wasn't a lot older than me when they met, and she was pregnant. Uncle Roy thought she was trash, and he was super against the marriage."

Why was he surprised? Everyone had their biases and prejudices. Just because Roy had been a thief didn't mean he couldn't be a snob.

Baby said, "He forgave my uncle Bert, but he never would acknowledge Patty was his great-niece. He always said she wasn't his blood."

"I see. Well, thank you."

Baby said, "Uncle Bert is... People get the wrong idea about him. But even after all those things Uncle Roy said about Cindy, he was the one who visited Uncle Roy in the hospital the most. He used to argue with Mommy about letting Uncle Roy's friends come and see him."

"Uncle Roy's friends?"

Baby said uncomfortably, "Gay people. Uncle Roy kept an apartment in Missoula, where he used to visit his gay friends. After he got sick and went into the hospital, Mommy wouldn't have any of those people around him. Uncle Bert said what did it matter? But it did to Mommy."

"What happened to the apartment in Missoula?" Jason asked.

She shrugged. "I think Uncle Bert and Cindy cleared it out. I don't know."

Jason said, "Thank you. You've been really helpful." He held up the locket. "And I'll see that this goes back to where it belongs."

She nodded sadly, turned, and walked away.

Jason watched her for a moment. He glanced at the locket, and he couldn't help smiling. Proof. The proof he had been waiting for.

The locket proved beyond a shadow of a doubt that Captain Roy Thompson's thefts were not limited to the altar piece and the paintings. He had sent the locket home too, which meant there was a very good chance every single one of the fifteen missing items on the Engelshofen Castle art-collection center's inventory list had been removed by Thompson and no other.

Well, maybe one other.

He dropped the locket in his pocket and headed for his car.

The gray, glass-paned door opened, and Jason held up the bottle of Patrón Estate Release tequila. "Is this a bad time?"

Doc's brows rose. "Not according to your friend there." He grinned and unlatched the screen, pushed it wide. "Come in. I was just having supper. You're welcome to join me."

"Thanks, I've already eaten," Jason lied.

He stepped past the bronze Indian chief doorstop and followed Doc down the black and white gallery of his glory days.

"The Screaming Eagles," Jason said. "Now that was a tough outfit. The 'tip of the spear,' right? First Allied soldiers to set foot into occupied France. You guys were in Bavaria in May '45. You drank wine and cognac from Hitler's own cellars."

Doc said, "You're sure one for trivia. Did you know Jimi Hendrix was with the 101st?"

"Which means you *were* in Bavaria at the same time as the 3rd Infantry Division. The same time as your old pal Captain Roy Thompson."

"Like the song says, it's a small, small world."

Doc led the way into the tidy kitchen. The table was set for one. Trout and potatoes were sizzling in butter in a frying pan on the stove.

"Fresh caught this morning. Do you like to fish, Agent West?" Doc asked.

"I do. I don't have much time for it these day, but yes. My grandfather taught me. He was in Bavaria around the same time as you and Captain Thompson."

Doc made a thoughtful sound, using a spatula to turn the fish over. "Is this that Emerson Harley fellow you were asking about the other day?"

"That's right. He was Deputy Chief with the Monuments, Fine Arts, and Archives program."

"A Monuments Man." Doc's smile was wry. He glanced at Jason. "I think I know where this is headed." He nodded at the table. "Have a seat. I'll fix our drinks."

Jason sat down at the table. A set of Delft-style windmill salt-and-pepper shakers sat on the polished walnut. He lifted the saltshaker and read the faint stamp: Occupied Japan. He put the saltshaker down.

Doc was busy pouring ice and tequila into the blender. "The secret to a great margarita is fresh juice."

Jason's gaze traveled idly around the well-scrubbed kitchen. The hardwood floor looked clean enough to eat off. He had been pretty sure of his theory when he'd arrived on Doc's doorstep, but now he was starting to wonder.

"Were you a combat medic? Is that where the nickname came from?"

Doc laughed. "Nope. The nickname came because of my sterling ability to give Jerry a taste of his own medicine."

"Ah."

Doc turned on the blender. As the ice and liquid whirled around noisily, he studied Jason—and Jason studied him back.

Doc turned off the blender, poured the margarita mix into two sparkling glasses, and carried them to the table.

Jason took his glass, clinked rims.

Doc said, "Geronimo."

Jason sipped the cold, tangy liquid. He was not a huge fan of margaritas, but this was pretty good. The fresh juice did make a difference.

"Do you always have a batch of these ready to go?"

"Sure. Always Be Prepared. That's the 101st's motto."

Jason grinned. "Actually, that's the Boy Scouts' motto. The 101st's motto is Rendezvous with Destiny, isn't it?"

Doc considered. "Maybe it is," he agreed. He sipped his drink, then swallowed the rest in a gulp.

Jason followed suit.

"Another?" Doc inquired.

"Yep."

Doc made another batch, carried the pitcher to the table, and refilled their glasses. "I don't care for salt. At my age, it's a bad idea. And I don't want you thinking I'm trying to poison you."

Jason laughed. "Nah. You wouldn't make the mistake of trying to get fancy. You'd just hit me over the head with that bronze doorstop before I left."

Doc laughed too. "I like you kid. You're a pistol." He downed his drink, said briskly, "Let's have another, and I'll tell you what you want to know."

# Chapter Seventeen

The funny thing was Jason did most of the talking.

He started out discussing his case—and his darkest suspicions (which amused the hell out of Doc)—and somehow wound his way to talking about his grandfather and how important it had seemed to clear his name and protect his legacy, when the truth was Emerson Harley would have brushed all that tarnished-reputation stuff aside as *nonsensical bullshit*. One of his favorite phrases. Emerson Harley would have said the successful work he had done during the war was all the legacy any man needed.

"No," Doc said solemnly, raising his glass and staring Jason in the eye. "Nope. He'd have said *you're* his legacy."

Of course, Doc was outdrinking Jason two-to-one at that point.

"I don't know why Roy's story changed over the years," Doc admitted. "I don't know why he did half the things he did. It wasn't to get rich. He didn't care that much about money. He didn't sell any of the treasures. I can tell you that. He'd be mad as hell to know they're being sold off now. He did give things to people. He gave his mama that pair of emerald earrings. Now what was she supposed to do with those? A nice little church-going lady like her? I think she wore them to Christmas once and gave them to the Goodwill."

Jason choked on his drink and started coughing.

Doc shrugged. "Roy was pretty upset, but I don't know what he expected. I do know why he thought he couldn't give the things back. There just wasn't any way without it coming out what he'd done. No way was *that* going to happen."

"Where are the rest of the paintings?" Jason asked.

"I have no idea where they are now. I can tell you where they were at one time. There's a shed at the back of Roy's property with a trapdoor leading down into a basement. He had that room all fixed up like his own personal little museum."

"This is the property Quilletta inherited?"

"That's right. She and Roy were always thick as thieves." Doc snorted.

"One of them killed de Haan."

"No." Doc shook his head. "I can see why you might think so, but no. There's not enough backbone in all of them put together."

Jason let the backbone comment slide. He didn't think hitting a man from behind required a lot of courage.

He told Doc about his belief that Police Chief Sandford was somehow involved, and Doc shot that down too.

"No damn way. There's no way Roy included Sandford in his will. He couldn't stand Sandford. Never liked him. Thought he was a bully and a cheat."

"Well, where did he form that opinion? Maybe that's a clue right there."

Doc shook his head. "I don't think so. No."

Jason was not drinking nearly as much as Doc, but he was drinking—clearly—because then he told Doc about the shootout at the Big Sky Guest Ranch and his suspicion that Bert had phoned Sandford even before the bullets started flying. From there he got onto the topic of Russell and his difficulty in dealing with having killed someone, and his own fear of getting shot again.

"You'd be stupid *not* to be afraid," Doc told him. "Were you crying and pissing yourself?"

"What? No. Of course not."

"Then you were fine. You were doin' *great*."

And somehow—so maybe he'd had more to drink than he realized—from there Jason got onto the topic of Sam and his own mistakes in their relationship.

"He let *you* down," Doc said, slurring ever so slightly. "You came to him for help, and he turned on you and threw you to the wolves. Did he help you? *No.* Forget about him. Heartless bastard. I *hate* sonofabitchin' heartless bastards."

Jason's phone rang, and they both blinked at it like phones were a new invention.

Jason picked his cell up, peered at the ID display.

"I should take this."

Doc waved him off and gloomily considered his empty glass.

Jason stepped out into the backyard. The cool night air felt good against his flushed face. The air smelled of flowers. A fountain chattered softly from the center of a rock garden. Moonlight gilded the treetops, blanching the roses and other blooms. He could hear the sound of the neighbors' television drifting over the wooden fence.

He clicked to accept the call.

"Hey," J.J. greeted him. "Maybe you're not as crazy as I thought you were."

"Thank you for calling," Jason said. "I'm sure I'll sleep better tonight."

"Yeah, but I know the connection between Sandford and the Thompsons. Well, Quilletta and Sandford."

"What's the connection?"

"They used to be a hot item in this town."

"When?"

"About eight years ago. They were having a not-so-secret affair. It broke up Sandford's first marriage and it's probably part of the reason the Winter Squash King ran off with his girlfriend."

Jason said slowly, "That's the second husband, right? The one you haven't been able to get in contact with?"

"Right. I mean, eight years is a long time ago, and the affair has been over for nearly that long. But there *is* a connection. You were right."

"Are you out with Martinez?"

"Yep. How do you think I learned all this?"

Where would law enforcement be without local gossip?

"Okay. This is helpful."

"I *know* it's helpful," J.J. said. "I just *told* you it was helpful."

Maybe J.J. had had a drink or two himself that evening.

"Right. Well, we'll figure out our game plan tomorrow."

"You're welcome," J.J. said and hung up.

Jason walked into the house and found what appeared to an old-fashioned hatbox sitting in the middle of the table.

"This is what you wanted," Doc told him. "I'm not saying your answers are in here, but any answers in here will be yours." He nodded solemnly.

Jason nodded too, because at the moment it did seem to make a lot of sense.

"I should be going," he said. "I want to check something out while I'm thinking about it."

"You have a rendezvous with destiny," Doc pronounced.

"I don't know. Maybe?"

"Go east and take the first right onto South 8th Avenue," Doc advised. "Follow that for about .19 of a mile. The house will be on your right. Light green with dark green trim. Peaked roof. It's sitting on three lots. The shed is in the back. There's alley access. That's going to be your best bet."

"Got it."

"You can let yourself out."

Jason nodded. He retraced his steps down the hallway with the black and white gallery of Doc's life in pictures, stepped over the Indian chief doorstop he'd suspected Doc might try to brain him with, unlocked the door, then closed it behind him.

A familiar SUV with official police insignia was parked in front of Quilletta's house.

Every light in the place seemed to be on, and Jason could see right through the ruffly kitchen curtains to where Quilletta was crying at the table while Chief Sandford stood over her, waving his arms and shouting.

Keeping an eye on the two framed in the window, Jason pulled his cell phone out.

"Jesus Christ. You have horrible timing," J.J. informed him.

"Where are you?"

"The last place I want to hear from you."

"Oh. Sorry. The thing is, I think I need some backup here. I'm over at Roy's old house. I got a tip that the paintings are in a shed basement in the back of the property."

"Are you fucking kidding me?" J.J. demanded, now sounding fully awake and sober. "You can't go in there. You don't have a warrant."

"I know. Before we try to get a warrant, I want to see if there's even any point. Thompson may have disposed of everything but the altar piece and the two paintings."

J.J. was silent for a moment. "You know, this isn't how it's done."

"I know."

"It's unlawful entry, West. At the *least*. If you're caught breaking in, your career is over."

"My career is over anyway. If there's any chance of getting that treasure back, I'm willing to take it."

"What are you—? And if I'm caught, *my* career is over too!"

"Don't get caught. Are you coming or not?"

"You *asshole*. Yes, I'm coming! Don't step foot on that goddamned property till I get there."

The shed was locked. That was not a surprise.

The surprise was that the key was on top of the door-frame. All Jason had to do was reach up, feeling along the frame until he found the chill bite of metal.

He glanced over his shoulder. He could still hear Sandford's voice floating down the unlit garden, but trees blocked his view of the house. Sprinklers were shooting across the lawn, water drops turning silver in the moonlight as they bounced off shrubs and grass.

Jason unlocked the door. It opened on soundless hinges.

He stepped into the dark interior, switched on his high-powered pocket flashlight. The beam played over what appeared to be an artist's studio. An easel stood near the window. Blank canvases rested against one wall. Painted canvases leaned against the opposite wall. From what he could see, the blank canvases looked to be more valuable.

Something glinted in the spotlight created by his flashlight. A pair of round spectacles lying by the floorboard near the door.

His heart jumped. He took his phone out and snapped a photo. He did not move the spectacles. He was doing his best not to move or touch anything he didn't have to.

A Bokhara red rug was positioned in the center of the room. Jason knelt, flipped the rug back, and the trapdoor was right there.

His heart pounded. If this was what he thought it was?

This was probably how Carter had felt, stepping into Tutankhamun's tomb. Or Marcel Ravidat falling down the hole that had turned into the Lascaux caves.

He felt for the recessed handle, lifted it up, and raised the door. It opened without so much as a squeak. A cold gust of funky air rose up. His nostrils twitched at the smoky smell of faded turpentine, varnish, walnut oil, old wood…and something weird, as bitter as wormwood.

*What the hell was that?*

Cement steps led down into what appeared to be a large and very dark basement. The reach of moonlight did not stretch beyond the top of the steps.

Jason shone his flashlight down the stairs. He could not see anything in the gloom.

He started down.

When he reached the bottom, he directed his flashlight beam around the long, rectangular room. His heart nearly stopped as he took in walls lined with gold-framed paintings.

A lot more than nine paintings.

Scenes from myth and legend and everyday life. Laughing faces, haunted faces, abstract faces. Pageantry, poverty, and everything in between. The story of mankind told in the poetry of paint and canvas.

"Jesus…" he whispered. A lump filled his throat. His eyes stung. It was humbling. Standing there in the presence of these both familiar and unfamiliar masterpieces, he was almost overcome by a sense of reverence.

Slowly, he circled the room, scanning its contents, and two things immediately struck him.

One was a wooden-framed painting placed on a decorative display easel—a work of art in its own right. A young man with long dark hair was washing his hands in front of a stained-glass window.

The other thing that stood out for Jason was the skeleton tied to a chair.

# CHAPTER EIGHTEEN

Proof that he was Emerson Harley's grandson, Jason went to examine the painting first.

Partly that was because he assumed the skeleton was a vintage medical skeleton. Maybe Roy's taste for antiquities stretched to the macabre.

Partly that was because… Vermeer.

He felt almost dizzy gazing at the familiar face of the man in the portrait. Familiar because it was the same model who had posed for *The Astronomer* and *The Geographer*. Same absorbed expression, same long, sensitive face, same expressive hands. He wore a similar scholarly dressing gown of green-blue. The room was the same as in the other portraits. Same corner cupboard, same twin globes—one celestial, one terrestrial—but the desk with its maps and books had been replaced by a table with a gleaming basin and jug. A Grecian-style statue, an armillary sphere atop a painted trunk, and a telescope crowded the background.

They had been wrong. Both he and Hans had guessed wrong. Vermeer had used the composition of *The Astronomer* and *The Geographer* rather than that of *The Love Letter* or *A Maid Asleep*. Instead, he had framed the painting so that the viewer seemed to be standing right outside the half-door, gazing into the room at a particular and unexpectedly private moment.

Belatedly, Jason remembered the skeleton—remembered why that skeleton was only too relevant, and remembered why it was highly unlikely to be a medical skeleton.

He turned reluctantly from the painting.

"*Throw your piece out and come up with your hands out.*"

Sandford's voice boomed overhead.

Jason instinctively jumped for the deep shadows along the near wall. He knew from trying to look down from above, that even if Sandford turned on the lights, he would not be able to see him from that angle.

"You're making this harder than it has to be," Sandford said.

"I could say the same to you," Jason called back. He moved quickly along the wall, grabbed an antique six-foot art pole, and jabbed it at the foot holding the door up.

The trapdoor slammed down with a loud bang.

Quilletta's voice murmured dismay from overhead.

"You're not getting out of there," Sandford yelled. "I don't know what good you think that does."

He opened fire at the trapdoor. Light from above pierced through the bullet holes.

Quilletta began screaming. Jason yelled, "*Are you out of your fucking mind?* Do you know what's down here?"

"*You're* down there!"

"Those paintings are worth millions," Quilletta cried. "You can't start shooting in there."

"I'm not going to jail for a bunch of paintings," Sandford said. "I should never have agreed to help you the first time. It never ends. Every goddamned time I turn around, there's a new one to get rid of."

Quilletta was talking through her sobs, but Jason couldn't make out what she was saying.

Sandford shot twice more. A bullet ricocheted off the floor and hit the wall a foot or two from Jason. A second bullet knocked a painting off the wall. Quilletta started screaming again, and Sandford told her to shut up.

Jason began to swear. He did not want to die, but he could not just stand here and let this treasure trove of priceless art be destroyed. He racked his brain, but there was nothing like bullets flying to ruin your concentration.

His best bet was to hold them off as long as possible. Three lots or not, her neighbors were surely going to hear all the screaming and shooting. And J.J. had to be close to arrival.

"Come out of there, or I'll fill that fucking room with bullets." Sandford added in afterthought, "I just want to talk to you."

Jason gave a shaky laugh. Sure. Just a friendly chat.

When he didn't respond, Sandford began firing through the splintered Swiss cheese of the trapdoor again.

Sandford stopped firing. "Fine. That's the way you want it? How about this? We'll lock you in and set the shed on fire."

"*Wait*," Jason shouted. "Wait. I'm coming up."

"Throw your piece out first. Then lock your hands behind your head and climb out slowly." Sandford added, "Quilletta is going to open the door, so you're only going to shoot her. And if you shoot her, I'll plug you anyway."

Quilletta protested. Sandford snarled, "Open the god-damned door. He's not going to shoot you."

Jason took a couple of calming breaths. Sandford wasn't going to shoot him the minute he raised his head up. This wasn't Whac-A-Mole. He'd want to know what Jason knew, right? And who else knew it.

Although the chief did not seem overly weighed down in the logic department.

Quilletta fumbled with the door, and it slowly rose a few inches.

"Throw your gun out," Sandford commanded.

Jason put his Glock on safety, tossed it out. He heard it thump down, heard the ugly scrape as it was kicked aside.

"Come on up."

Jason's mouth was dry as a wool blanket. His heart was stuttering against his collarbone.

"I'm coming up," he said, and tugged up the left leg of his jeans.

Quilletta pulled the trapdoor open and jumped to the side. Sandford stood directly in front of the opening. He leveled his weapon, smiling. Jason started slowly up the stairs. The light was unexpectedly bright. He winced, stumbled, and went down on his left leg, drawing his backup Glock from his ankle holster and springing up like a jack-in-the-box, shoving his pistol in Sandford's astonished face.

"Twitch and I'll kill you," Jason gasped. "And if that Vermeer has a hole in it, I'll kill you anyway."

Sandford jammed his weapon in Jason's chest, and felt the resistance of Kevlar. Jason shook his head. *Been there, done that,* and he was so mad he didn't care anyway.

He saw Sandford's eyes flicker as he recognized the truth.

"Drop your weapon," Martinez shouted from the doorway of the shed. "Do it now." She filled the doorway in perfect firing stance, despite the fact that she seemed to be wearing a short cotton nightie with a WordGirl pattern over her jeans and boots.

"He's not kidding," J.J. leaned through the open window, leveling his Glock. "Take it from me. He has no sense of humor when it comes to art."

* * * * *

"You're not staying for the party?" J.J. asked.

"Nope."

"You're flying back this afternoon?" J.J. said.

"Yep."

"I mean, the party *is* kind of in our honor."

Sort of. Martinez's presence the evening before had given the Bozwin RA right to claim credit in the recovery of what local papers were hailing as "the stunning recovery of a record-breaking haul of art and treasures looted by the Nazis." But mostly the party—thrown by Special Agent Travis Petty— was to celebrate the drawing to a (what would surely be) successful conclusion of the Deerlodge Destroyer case. In other words, two celebrations for the price of one bar tab.

Jason said, "You'll have to do the honors for both our... honors."

He was on his way to the airport—only stopping by the Bozwin RA to make sure he hadn't left anything—any thing that was still his to take—and to say his farewells.

"You're not going to explain to me what's actually going on?"

"You know what's going on. Quilletta Thompson killed her second husband eight years ago in a fit of rage before he could run off with a girl he'd met online. Her uncle Roy and then-boyfriend Police Chief Amos Sandford helped her cover it up and hide the body."

Not like they hadn't been over it a million times last night with Bozwin PD, the Gallatin County Sheriff's Office, SAC Phillips, and finally a bleary-eyed conference call at dawn with the top brass from the SLC Field Office.

"Which de Haan stumbled over."

"Yes. Unfortunately, de Haan tried to do the same thing I did last night—and also tripped the silent alarm. Quilletta trotted down there with her great-uncle's trusty marble bookend and bashed him over the head when he was climbing out of the basement."

Which turned out to be a lot more effective than the screaming and shooting engaged in by Chief Sandford. Granted, by then Sandford had been at his breaking point.

Welcome to the club.

"That part I know," J.J. said. "And Chief Sandford had to help her *again* by moving the body because if the first crime was ever discovered, his involvement would be known and he'd be ruined."

"That's pretty much it." And Jason was pretty much tired of the whole stupid, sordid scenario.

"It never was about the art?"

"No."

"Why the hell didn't she just admit she had the rest of the treasure? She could have cut a deal then and there. If she hadn't lied, de Haan would never have started poking around—and then *you* wouldn't have started poking around..."

"Greed, I guess. She thought she could hang on to her secrets and millions of dollars' worth of art as well. Anyway."

Jason closed the desk drawer. He was just stalling. Delaying the moment he had to say goodbye to Sam.

Maybe J.J. read his thoughts because he said, "I still don't get why you're in such a panic to leave. And why is Salt Lake's ACT taking possession of the art *we* found? Why are we suddenly off this case? Why are you and Kennedy not speaking to each other?"

"We're speaking to each other. I'm about to go tell him goodbye. As for the rest of it, don't look a surprise three-day weekend in the mouth. You don't have to be in LA until Tuesday, so take advantage of that."

J.J. scowled. "You know, you're not fooling me, West. You spent nearly two hours on the phone with George this morning and then another three hours with Kapszukiewicz."

Jason couldn't think of an answer.

"They're not going to—no way are they going to *can* you after you found a goddamned Vermeer. Not to mention all those other paintings." J.J. added uncertainly, "Are they?"

"I don't know," Jason admitted. "I hope not."

He had never heard Karan raise her voice before, but he'd heard it plenty this morning. And George... George had even used the word *disappointed*; twice.

It hurt. A lot.

He hadn't meant to say even that much. J.J. looked horrified. "Jesus Christ. Are you kidding? You're *not* kidding?"

"I'm sure everything's fine," Jason lied. "And since I have to be in Washington on Monday morning—"

"Uh, it's a shorter flight from here than L.A. You wouldn't have to miss the party. Free booze and BBQ on a wraparound deck overlooking the Gallatin River."

Yeah. Hosted bar notwithstanding, about the only thing Jason could picture enjoying *less* was being shot to death in Roy Thompson's underground museum-slash-tomb.

"I'm reeeeeally not in a party mood," he said.

J.J. studied him, said after a moment, "I told you he was an asshole. Many times I warned you."

"Seriously. Don't."

J.J. shrugged. "See you...Tuesday?"

Jason nodded, his smile wry. "Bright and early."

If only to clear out his desk.

Jason rapped on the doorframe of Sam's temporary office.

Sam, standing by the window and gazing out at the parking lot, glanced over, and Jason saw something like surprise flash through his eyes.

"I just came to say goodbye," Jason said.

Sam nodded. He left the window, walking toward Jason—but then stopped beside his desk. "You're not staying for the party?"

"No. I need to get back."

Sam didn't say anything.

Jason hesitated. What the hell was there left to say, really?

But...if a thing was worth having, it was worth fighting for. Right? And while this was starting to feel hopeless, they had come so far.

Or was that his imagination too?

He stepped into the office, closed the door.

"I just wanted to say..." He drew in a sharp breath, let it out slowly, evenly. "I'm sorry I turned out not to be who you thought I was. I'm sorry you think I can't be trusted."

"I wish it were that simple." Sam was frowning bleakly into some distance Jason couldn't see, his right index finger absently, nervously tapping the manila folder beneath his hand in a soundless tattoo.

"Why *isn't* it that simple?" Jason asked. "Jesus Christ, Sam. Did it ever occur to you this isn't about *you*?"

Emotion flashed across Sam's face. Doubt. Affront. Confusion.

Three expressions he'd rarely—ever?—seen on Kennedy's face.

Jason said, "I get that I put you in an awkward position. I get that you disapprove of my actions. Does it really not make any difference that I didn't attempt to cover up the facts of the case? That I did everything I could to keep my investigation fair and unbiased? That I conducted myself as I would have in any other case?"

Sam said dryly, "By conducting yourself as you would in any other case, you mean by gambling your life and taking unnecessary risks?"

"Wow. That's...pretty unfair. And that's not what we're talking about."

"No," Sam agreed. "But since we're on the subject of last night, why the hell didn't you let me know what you were planning?"

*Were* they on the subject of last night? It seemed they were. Jason was going to have whiplash at this rate.

"It was more impulse than plan."

Sam rephrased, "Why didn't you call me when you knew what you were going to do?"

*Really?* Did Sam *really* not understand this? Could he *possibly* be this oblivious? This emotionally out-of-touch? He was so good at reading other people, at analyzing what made people tick. He *had* to know what he was doing.

"Sam, I'll never ask you for help again as long as I live. I'd die first." Jason wasn't angry. He said it matter-of-factly.

Sam's eyes narrowed. He smiled without humor, and said, "That's a little dramatic."

Was it? Because Jason meant it. He wasn't going to forget that he had turned to Sam for help—and Sam had turned on *him*.

"Well, hey, not the first time you've told me that."

He waited, but Sam simply continued to stand there frowning at him.

That wasn't normal, right? It wasn't just him; this was not the way most people would behave in this situation.

Not that Jason had previous experience with this situation.

When it was clear Sam was not going to add anything, Jason shrugged. "Okay. Well, that was it. That was my whole speech. I don't know what more I can say. It doesn't seem to matter."

Nothing.

Emotion squeezed Jason's heart so hard, he thought it would simply stop beating.

He said—and his voice shook, but he forced himself to talk past it, "I love you, and I think you do love me. As much as you're capable. But there's something…cold about you. That you can turn this off and on at will. I'm not saying I'm great at relationships either, but I do know you don't get to take *breaks* from loving someone. And the fact that you do, that you *can* just…turn me off. Shut me out. That it always has to be your rules or nothing. I can't do it anymore." He let out a long, shuddery breath. "Even if I wanted to. I can't. I just can't take it."

Some emotion flashed through Sam's eyes. Another expression Jason had never seen. *Fear?* No way. And yet… Sam hesitated, opened his mouth—and someone knocked on the door. His face tightened with frustration. He pressed his lips together tightly.

Jason glanced out the sidelight and spotted Petty with a stack of folders. Because of course. *Of course*, it would be goddamned Special Agent Travis Petty waiting eagerly in the wings. Well, good luck, asshole. He plastered a determined smile on his face, opened the door.

Petty offered a quick, apologetic grin. "Hey. Sorry to interrupt."

"Hey, nothing to interrupt," Jason returned.

He stepped past Petty and kept walking.

# CHAPTER NINETEEN

The sound of doves cooing beneath the pergola on the side of the house reminded Jason of Montana's pornographic pigeons and the last morning he and Sam had been together. Really together.

*Don't.*

Don't start down that road.

Because right now he was okay. He was happy to be home. Grateful for peace and quiet and...normalcy. He had speed-read through Roy Thompson's letters on the flight back from Bozwin, and he was feeling...at peace.

As he had hoped—and feared—his grandfather's name did pop up in Thompson's correspondence. At first Thompson had been proud of being assigned to help protect the treasure of Engelshofen Castle. He had liked working with Emerson Harley, whom he considered an equal in intellect and sophistication. But Deputy Chief Harley had reprimanded him twice on—according to Thompson—trivial but unspecified matters.

After that Thompson's tone had changed.

Jason could guess, but was never going to know for sure why Thompson had tried to implicate Emerson Harley in his thefts—and Jason had not been able to find any hard physical evidence that his grandfather had *not* been complicit—but he was okay with allowing people to draw their own conclusions.

People would believe what they wanted to believe. Because that's how people were.

If he had to do it all over again... Well, he had made mistakes, big ones. Given the chance, he would try to learn from them and not repeat them.

He was not sure he would be given the chance. Not as far as his job went. Not as far as anything went.

But then, as far as "anything" went, he wasn't the only one who had made mistakes.

If he was not terminated on Monday, he was going to ask George for a little time off.

Time to pause and reflect, sure, but mostly time to fly to Amsterdam and speak with de Haan's Anna. He wanted her to know how important Hans's help had been—if anyone deserved credit for restoring that Vermeer to the world, it was him—and he wanted her to know how much Hans had wanted to keep his promise to her.

He dumped the contents of his luggage in the washing machine, wandered into the kitchen and opened the fridge, studying the fresh cartons of eggs and milk, the loaf of bread—his sister Charlotte doing what big sisters did.

Not that he was hungry, but one of his resolutions on the flight home had been to make a disciplined effort to opt for healthy choices. Eat more. Drink less. That would be a good start.

Someone tapped sharply on the glass window of the kitchen door, and he jumped—remembering instantly that

Jeremy Kyser might not really be dead, that he must not let his guard down.

Heart in mouth, he went to look out the window.

Sam frowned in at him.

They stared at each other through the glass, and for the first time Jason could remember, he was not glad to see Sam Kennedy on his doorstep.

For Sam to show up this fast, he had to have left the office within a few hours of Jason.

At a guess? He'd thought it all over, come to a logical conclusion, and was here to cross another chore off his Things To Do list. Jason opened the door, and managed to say coolly, "Delivering the bad news in person, I guess?"

"Yes." Sam looked grim. Tired and grim. He stopped, waiting, and Jason stepped back, waving him in with an *advance to the next square* motion.

Sam stepped inside. He was looking at Jason—only at Jason—and his expression seemed odd, watchful. "Jason, there isn't any easy way to say this. I've seen the DNA results, and Kyser is not dead."

Jason had been braced to hear something else entirely, so that was almost—*almost*—a relief.

"I see."

"I...wanted you to know as soon as possible."

"Of course." Not his imagination. That was definitely a strange expression on Sam's face. "You want a drink? I'm pretty sure I need one."

Sam hesitated. "Thank you."

Jason gave a short laugh and went to the kitchen cupboard where he kept a bottle of Canadian Club in the hope that Sam might someday surprise drop by. And see, he'd finally got his wish.

He got out two short glasses, dropped a couple of ice cubes in with a *clink*, and poured the whisky, all the while conscious of the fact that Sam was still standing by the door—the better to make a quick escape?—silently watching him.

Jason said at random, "This isn't really a surprise. I never thought he was dead."

He handed Sam his drink, taking care not to brush fingers. "Geronimo." He swallowed a mouthful of whisky and winced at the burn.

Jesus. Canadian Club was god-awful stuff. That alone should have warned him off Sam.

"No, you didn't," Sam said. "And I didn't have to come here in person to tell you this."

"I know. You're going to miss the celebration party and the wraparound dick."

Sam made a choked sound.

Jason stared at him. "So why *did* you come, Sam?"

Sam stared down at his drink like he didn't know how it had appeared in his hand. He tossed it back in one gulp.

"Okay, then," Jason said.

"I know why," Sam said. He was looking at Jason with a kind of pained, inarticulate… expectation. Expectation of *what*? Understanding? Jason did *not* understand.

"You know why what?" Jason asked.

"I prefer to know what's going to happen."

"Uh, I think we all do."

"No." Sam shook his head. "With Ethan...I always knew what he would do, what he thought. I didn't always like it, but I could always predict it. I can't do that with you. I *don't* always know what you're thinking, and I *can't* always predict what you're going to do."

"Well, that's how it is," Jason protested. "That's how it works. I don't know what you're going to say or do either."

"But I *need* that." At Jason's incredulous expression, Sam closed his eyes, seemed to struggle for the words. "I mean, I'm used to that. I don't like feeling vulnerable. I don't like feeling things are out of control. And when you lie to me—"

"Jesus Christ," Jason said. "I didn't *lie* to you. I came to you for *help*—"

"And I let you down," Sam cut in. His eyes were dark with emotion. "I'm sorry. I feel... I regret it. I wish I could do it over. You were right this morning. It wasn't about me. I should never have made it about me. Or about us."

Jason had not expected an apology. Had certainly not expected Sam to try to work through where it had all gone wrong for them. But maybe he should have because Sam was nothing if not analytical. Even if it was over for them, Sam would want to understand why—and, being Sam—would probably want Jason to understand why too.

Sam said, "But where you're wrong is about turning you off, shutting you out. I can't. Even if I wanted to. And I *don't* want to. You're the best thing in my life. Maybe the best thing that ever happened to me. You're my first thought in the morning and my last thought at night. That's the truth.

I'm *not* cold. Not where you're concerned. If I could get a little distance—"

"*Distance* is not the answer in a relationship. For God's sake. Communication is the answer. Even *I* know that much."

Sam put his glass down and drew Jason into his arms. Jason didn't try to pull away, but he didn't surrender either. He still felt bruised, uncertain.

Sam kissed his temple, the side of his mouth, soft and apologetic, taking nothing for granted. "I'm sorry. I don't mean to hurt you. I never want to hurt you."

But he sure had a knack for it.

Jason said wearily, "I know. But you didn't want this relationship." He'd had plenty of time to think on the flight too. "There's no secret about that. You've been fighting it since day one."

"I want this relationship more than anything."

Sam said it so simply, so sincerely, it was impossible not to believe him—and Jason wanted to believe him. So much. Too much. His throat closed, and he shook his head.

Sam bent his head, said against his ear, "It doesn't matter how it started or what I once felt. It doesn't matter that it scares the hell out of me. I want it, and I'm willing to do whatever you want. Whatever will make you happy. If I can. I'm not saying I won't make mistakes or screw it up again, but if you could just remember that however…fucked up I seem, however fucked up I am… I love you."

Jason wiped impatiently at his eyes. "I feel like we've been here before, and I just…can't keep doing this."

He felt Sam's swallow. Felt Sam's pain without having to look at him. How could you know someone so well—and not at all?

It was frightening that so much of his happiness depended on another person.

But wasn't that what Sam struggled with too?

Sam whispered, "Okay, West. Whatever you want. I mean that. If you want me to go, I will."

Jason closed his eyes. Yes or no? If they were just going to end up here again in a couple of months, wouldn't it be easier to get it over with now?

Yes, it would be easier. It was called giving up, and that was always easier. Whether it was art or love, anything worth having was worth fighting for.

Jason opened his eyes. "Don't go."

Jason West and Sam Kennedy
will return in  Winter 2020 in
# THE MOVIE-TOWN MURDERS

*Keep reading! If you liked*
**The Monument Men Murders**,
*you might like this excerpt form the first book
in the Dangerous Ground series.*

# DANGEROUS
# GROUND

# Chapter One

The nose of the red and white twin engine Baron 58 was crunched deep into the bottom of the wooded ravine. Mud and debris covered the cockpit windows. One wing had been sheared off when the plane crashed through the surrounding pines, knocking three of them over. The other wing was partially buckled beneath the craft. The tail of the plane had broken off and lay several yards down the ravine.

Taylor mopped his face on the flannel sleeve of his shirt. Ten thousand feet up in the High Sierras, the sun was still plenty warm despite the chill spring air.

Behind him, Will said, "Either the pilot was unfamiliar with the terrain or he didn't have a lot of experience with mountain flying. Out here, avoiding box canyons is one of the first things you learn."

"Take a look at this," Taylor said, and Will made his way to him across the rocky, uneven slope. Taylor pointed to the fuselage. "You see those registration numbers?"

"N81BH." Will's blue eyes met Taylor's. "Now why does that sound so familiar?"

Taylor grinned. "It's the plane used in that Tahoe casino heist last year."

Will whistled, long and low.

"Yeah," agreed Taylor. Just for a moment he let his gaze linger on the other man's lean, square-jawed features. Will's hair, brown and shining in the sun, fell boyishly into his eyes. He hadn't shaved in three days, and the dark stubble gave him a rugged, sexy look—very different from the normal nine to five Will. Not that they exactly worked nine to five at the Bureau of Diplomatic Security.

Will's gaze held his for a moment, and Taylor looked away, focusing on the plane's registration numbers again.

"What'd they get away with again?" Will asked in a making conversation kind of voice. "Something in the neighborhood of 2.3 million, was it?"

"That and murder," Taylor said grimly. "They shot two sheriff's deputies making their getaway." These days he was touchy about law enforcement officers getting gunned down.

"Doesn't look like they got away far." Will moved toward the open door of the plane. He hopped lightly up onto the broken wing, and for a moment Taylor felt a twinge of envy. He was still moving slowly after his own shooting six weeks ago; sometimes he felt like he was never going to get it all back: the strength, the speed—the confidence—he had always taken for granted. He felt old at thirty-one.

He walked toward the broken off tail piece, and Will—only half-joking—called, "Watch out for snakes, MacAllister."

"You had to say that, didn't you, Brandt?" Taylor threw back. He studied the rim of the ravine. It had been winter when three masked men with automatic weapons robbed the Black Wolf Casino on the Nevada border of Lake Tahoe. They had fled to the nearby airport, hijacked a plane, and disappeared into the snowy December night.

Local law enforcement had theorized the Beechcraft Baron crashed in the High Sierras, but the weather and the terrain had inhibited searchers. It was clear to Taylor now that even under the best conditions, it would have been just about impossible to spot the little plane tucked away in the crevice of this mountainside.

He glanced back, but Will had vanished inside the wrecked plane. He could hear the eerie creak and groan of the aircraft as Will moved around inside.

Taylor worked his way around the crash site. Not their area of expertise, of course, but he knew what to look for.

Scattered engine parts and broken glass were strewn everywhere. A couple of seats had been thrown clear and were relatively intact. There was a weathered plank of wood that must have originally been a table or a desk, and some broken light fixtures and vinyl parts of storage bins. The plane could have carried five passengers in addition to the pilot. The casino had been hit by three bandits; the fourth had been driving the getaway car that sped them to Truckee Tahoe Airport. Four people would have inevitably left DNA evidence, but the crash site was four months old and contaminated by the elements and wildlife. He glanced around at the sound of Will's boots on the loose rock.

Will said, "The pilot's inside. No one else."

That was no surprise. The initial investigation had cleared the pilot of involvement in the robbery; if he'd been alive, he would have contacted the authorities. Taylor thought it over. "No sign there were any passengers on board when she went down."

"What about an incriminating black tie?" Will referred to the famous narrow black necktie that legendary hijacker D.B.

Cooper left on the Boeing 727 he jumped out of way back in 1971.

"Not so much as a stray sock."

"Then I guess they weren't doing laundry up there," Will remarked, and Taylor drew a blank.

"You know how one sock always gets lost—forget it." It was a lame joke, but once Taylor would have known instantly what Will meant. Once Taylor would have laughed. "Parachutes?" Will asked.

"No parachutes."

"None?"

"Doesn't look like it," Taylor said.

"Interesting. The pilot's got a bullet through his skull."

"Ah," said Taylor.

"Yep."

Their eyes met.

"Come take a look," Will invited, and Taylor followed him back to the front section of the plane.

Will sprang onto the wing, reaching a hand down for Taylor, and with a grimace, Taylor accepted his help, vaulting up beside him. The wing bobbed beneath their weight, and Will steadied him, hands on Taylor's waist for an instant.

Taylor moved away. Not that he minded Will's hands on him—there was nothing he'd have liked more than Will's hands on him—but this had nothing to do with attraction and everything to do with lack of confidence. A lack of confidence in Taylor being able to look after himself. Not that Will had said so, but it was clear to Taylor—and maybe it was clear to Will too, which might explain what the hell they were doing up in the High Sierras one week before Taylor was officially due to start back at work.

Because if they couldn't figure this out—get past it—they were through as a team. Regardless of the fact that so far no one had admitted there was even a problem.

"After you," Will said, waving him into the gloomy and rotting interior of the plane with exaggerated courtesy. Taylor gave him a wry smile and ducked inside.

"Jesus. Something's made itself right at home in here."

"Yeah. Maybe a marmot. Or a weasel. Something relatively small." Will's breath was warm against the back of Taylor's neck.

"Relatively small is good," Taylor muttered, and Will laughed.

"Unless it's a skunk."

Almost four years they'd been together: partners and friends—good friends—but maybe that was over now. Taylor didn't want to think so, but —

His boot turned on a broken door lever, and Will's hand shot out, steadying him. Taylor pulled away, just managing to control his impatience.

Yeah, that was the problem. Will didn't think Taylor was capable of taking two steps without Will there to keep an eye on him.

And that was guilt. Pure and simple. Not friendship, not one partner watching another partner's back, not even the normal overprotectiveness of one partner for his injured-in-the-line-of-duty opposite number. No, this was guilt because of the way Taylor felt about Will—because Will didn't feel the same. And somehow Will had managed to convince himself that that was part of the reason Taylor had stopped a bullet.

He clambered across the empty copilot's seat and studied the remains of the dead pilot slumped over the instrument dashboard control panel. The pilot's clothes were in rags, deteriorated and torn. Bacteria, insects, and animals had reduced the body to a mostly skeletal state. Not entirely skeletal, unfortunately, but Taylor had seen worse as a special agent posted in Afghanistan. He examined the corpse dispassionately, noting position, even while recognizing that animals had been at it. Some of the smaller bones of the hands and feet were missing.

"One bullet to the back of the head," he said.

"Yep," Will replied. "While the plane was still in flight."

Taylor glanced down at the jammed throttle. "And then the hijackers bailed out," he agreed. This part at least still worked between them. They still could work a crime scene with that single-mindedness that had earned the attention and approval of their superiors.

Not that they investigated many homicides at the Bureau of Diplomatic Security. Mostly they helped in the extradition of fugitives who fled the country, or ran interference for local law enforcement agencies with foreign police departments. But now and then they got to…get their feet wet. Some times were a little wetter than others. Taylor rubbed his chest absently.

"In the middle of the night and in the middle of nowhere," Will said. "Hard to believe all four of them made it out of these mountains safely. FBI and the local law were all over these woods within twenty-four hours."

"Yeah, but it was snowing, remember."

"Those guys are trained."

"They missed the plane."

"The plane wasn't making for the main highway."

"Maybe the bad guys were local," Taylor said. "Maybe they knew the terrain."

"Wasn't the prevailing theory, was it?"

"No." He backed out of the cockpit, and Will did it again—rested his hand on Taylor's back to stabilize him—although Taylor's balance was fine, physically and emotionally.

He gritted his jaw, biting back anything that would widen the rift between them. Will's friendship was better than nothing, right? And there had been a brief and truly hellish period when he thought he'd lost that, so…shut up and be grateful, yeah?

Yeah.

Will jumped down to the ground and reached up a hand. Taylor ignored the hand, and dropped down beside him—which jarred his rib cage and hurt like fuck. He did his best to hide the fact.

"More likely what's left of 'em is scattered through these woods," Will commented, and Taylor grimaced.

"There's a thought."

"Imagine jumping out of a plane into freezing rain and whatever that headwind was? Eighteen knots. Maybe more."

"Maybe someone was waiting for them on the ground."

Will nodded thoughtfully. "Two and an almost-half million divides nicely between five."

Taylor grunted. Didn't it just? Kneeling by his pack, he unzipped it, dug through his clothes and supplies, searching for something on which he could note the crash site coordinates. It was sheer luck they'd stumbled on it this time. He found the small notebook he'd tossed in, fished further and found a pen, pulling the cap off with his teeth. He squinted up at the anvil-shaped cliff to the right of the canyon. The sun was starting to sink in the sky. He rose.

Will moved next to him, looking over his shoulder, and just that much proximity unsettled Taylor. It took effort not to move away, turn his back. Will smelled like sunshine and flannel and his own clean sweat as he brushed against Taylor's arm, frowning down at Taylor's diagram.

"What's that supposed to be? A chafing dish?"

Taylor pointed the pen. "It's that…thing. Dome or whatever you call it."

"If you say so, Picasso." Will unfolded his map. "Let me borrow your pen."

Taylor handed his pen over, and Will circled a spot on the map, before folding it up again, and shoving it in the back pocket of his desert camo pants.

"Well, hell," he said, "I guess we should start back down, notify the authorities we found their missing aircraft."

Will looked at him inquiringly, and Taylor nodded. That was the logical thing to do, after all. But he wasn't happy about it. Three days into their "vacation" they weren't any closer to bridging the distance yawning between them—and it would be a long time before they had this kind of opportunity again. By then it might be too late. Whereas this plane had been sitting here for over four months; would another four days really make a difference?

"Right. We'll rest up tonight and head back tomorrow then," Will added, after a moment.

Taylor directed a narrow look his way, but the truth was he *was* fatigued, and climbing in the dark would have been stupid even if he wasn't. So he nodded again, curtly, and tossed the notebook and diagram back into his pack.

* * * * *

Will was tired. Pleasantly tired. Taylor was exhausted. Not that he'd admit it, but Will could tell by the way he dropped down by the campfire while Will finished pitching their two-man tent.

One eye on Taylor, Will stowed their sleeping bags inside the Eureka Apex XT. He pulled Taylor's Therm-a-Rest sleeping pad out of his own backpack where he'd managed to stash it that morning without Taylor noticing, and spread it out on the floor of the tent. He opened the valve and left the pad inflating while he went to join Taylor at the fire.

"Hungry?"

"Always." Taylor's grin was wry—and so was Will's meeting it. Taylor ate like a horse—even in the hospital—although where he put it was anyone's guess. He was all whippy muscle and fine bones that seemed to be made out of titanium. It was easy to look at him and dismiss him as a threat, but anyone who'd ever tangled with him didn't make that mistake twice.

He was too thin now, though, which was why Will was carrying about three pounds more food in his pack than they probably needed. He watched Taylor feeding wood into the flames. In the firelight his face was all sharps and angles. His eyes looked almost black with fatigue—they weren't black, though, they were a kind of burnished green—an indefinable shade of bronze that reminded Will of old armor. Very striking with his black hair—Will's gaze lingered on Taylor's hair, on that odd single streak of silver since the shooting.

He didn't want to think about the shooting. Didn't want to think about finding Taylor in a dingy storeroom with his shirt and blazer soaked in blood—Taylor struggling for each anguished breath. He still had nightmares about that.

He said, talking himself away from the memory, "Well, monsieur, tonight zee specials are zee beef stroganoff, zee Mexican-style chicken, or zee lasagna with meat sauce."

"What won't they freeze-dry next?" Taylor marveled.

"Nothing. You name it, they'll freeze-dry it. We've got Neapolitan ice cream for dessert."

"You're kidding."

"Just like the astronauts eat."

"We pay astronauts to sit around drinking Tang and eating freeze-dried ice cream?"

"Your tax dollars at work." Will's eyes assessed Taylor. "Here." He shifted, pulled his flask out of his hip pocket, unscrewed the cap, and handed it to Taylor. "Before dinner cocktails."

"Cheers." Taylor took a swig and shuddered.

"Hey," Will protested. "That's Sam Houston bourbon. You know how hard that it is to find?"

"Yeah, I know. I bought you a bottle for Christmas year before last."

"That's right. Then you know just how good this is."

"Not if you don't like it." But Taylor was smiling—which was good to see. Not too many smiles between them since that last night at Will's house. And he wanted to think about that even less than he wanted to think about Taylor getting shot.

"Son, that bourbon will put hair on your chest," he said.

"Yeah, well, unlike you I prefer my bears in the woods."

There was a brief uncomfortable pause while they both remembered a certain naval officer, and then Taylor took another swig and handed the flask back to Will.

"Thanks."

Will grunted acknowledgment.

He thought about telling Taylor he hadn't seen Bradley since that god-awful night, but that was liable to make things worse—it would certainly confuse the issue, because regardless of what Taylor believed, the issue had never been Lieutenant Commander David Bradley.

Taylor put a hand to the small of his back, arching a little, wincing—and Will watched him, chewing the inside of his cheek, thinking it over. It was taking a while to get back into sync, that was all. It was just going to take a little time. Sure, Taylor was moody, a little distant, but he still wasn't 100 percent.

He was getting there, though. Getting there fast—because once Taylor put his mind to a thing, it was as good as done. Usually. When he started back at work he'd be stuck on desk duty for a couple of weeks, maybe even a month or so, but he'd be back in the field before long, and Will was counting the days. He missed Taylor like he'd miss his right arm. Maybe more.

Even now he was afraid—but there was no point thinking like that. They were okay. They just needed time to work through it. And the best way to do that was to leave the past alone.

"Warm enough?" he asked.

Taylor gave him a long, unfriendly look.

"Hey, just asking." Will rose. "I was going to get a sweater out of my bag for myself."

Taylor relaxed. "Yeah. Can you grab my fleece vest?"

Will nodded, and passing Taylor, took a swipe at the back of his head, which Taylor neatly ducked.

* * * * *

They had instant black bean soup and the Mexican-style chicken for dinner, and followed it up with the freeze-dried ice cream and coffee.

"It's not bad," Taylor offered, breaking off a piece of ice cream and popping it into his mouth.

Actually the ice cream wasn't that bad. It crunched when you put it into your mouth, then dissolved immediately, but Will said, "What do you know? You'll eat anything. If I didn't watch out you'd be eating poison mushrooms or poison berries or poison oak."

Taylor grinned. It was true; he was a city boy through and through. Will was the outdoors guy. He was the one who thought a week of camping and hiking was what they needed to get back on track; Taylor was humoring him by coming along on this trip. In fact, Will was still a little surprised Taylor had agreed. Taylor's idea of vacation time well spent was on the water and in the sun: renting a house boat—like they had last summer—or deep sea fishing—which Taylor had done on his own the year before.

"They never did arrest anyone in connection with that heist, did they?" Taylor said thoughtfully, after a few more minutes of companionable chewing.

"What heist?"

Taylor threw him an impatient look. "The robbery at the Black Wolf Casino."

"Oh. Not that I heard. I wasn't really following it." Taylor had a brain like a computer when it came to crimes and unsolved mysteries. When Will wasn't working, which, granted, was rarely, the last thing he wanted to do was think about crooks and crime—especially the ones that had nothing to do with them.

But Taylor was shaking his head like Will was truly a lost cause, so he volunteered, "There was something about the croupier, right? She was questioned a couple of times."

"Yeah. Questioned but never charged." He shivered.

Will frowned. "You all right?"

"*Jesus*, Brandt, will you give it a fucking *rest*!" And just like that, Taylor was unsmiling, stone-faced and hostile.

There was a short, sharp silence. "Christ, you can be an unpleasant bastard," Will said finally, evenly. He threw the last of his foil-wrapped ice cream into the fire, and the flames jumped, sparks shooting up with bits of blackened metal.

Taylor said tersely, "You want a more pleasant bastard for a partner, say the word."

The instant aggression caught Will off guard. Where the hell had it come from? "No, I don't want someone more pleasant," he said. "I don't want a new partner."

Taylor stared at the fire. "Maybe I do," he said quietly.

Will stared at him. He felt like he'd been sucker punched. Dopey and…off-kilter.

"Why'd you say that?" he asked finally into the raw silence between them.

He saw Taylor's throat move, saw him swallowing hard, and he understood that although Taylor had spoken on impulse, he meant it—and that he was absorbing that truth even as Will was.

"We're good together," Will said, not giving Taylor time to answer—afraid that if Taylor put it into words they wouldn't be able to go back from it. "We're…the best. Partners and friends."

He realized he was gripping his coffee cup so hard he was about to snap the plastic handle.

Taylor said, his voice low but steady, "Yeah. We are. But…it might be better for both of us if we were reteamed."

"Better for you, you mean?"

Taylor met his eyes. "Yeah. Better for me."

And now Will was getting angry. It took him a moment to recognize the symptoms because he wasn't a guy who got mad easily or often—and never at Taylor. Exasperated, maybe. Disapproving sometimes, yeah. But angry? Not with Taylor. Not even for getting himself shot like a goddamned wet-be-hind-the-ears recruit. But that prickling flush beneath his skin, that pounding in his temples, that rush of adrenaline—that was anger. And it was all for Taylor.

Will threw his cup away and stood up—aware that Taylor tensed. Which made him even madder—and Will was plenty mad already. "Oh, I get it," he said. "This is payback. This is you getting your own back—holding the partnership hostage to your hurt ego. This is all because I won't sleep with you, isn't it? That's what it's really about."

And Taylor said in that same infuriatingly even tone, "If that's what you want to think, go ahead."

Right. Taylor—the guy who jumped first and thought second, if at all; who couldn't stop shooting his mouth off if his life depended on it; who thought three months equaled the love of a lifetime—suddenly *he* was Mr. Cool and Reasonable. What a goddamn laugh. Mr. Wounded Dignity sitting there staring at Will with those wide, bleak eyes.

"What am I supposed to think?" Will asked, and it took effort to keep his voice as level as Taylor's. "That you're in love? We both know what this is about, and it ain't love, buddy boy. You just can't handle the fact that anyone could turn you down."

"Fuck you," Taylor said, abandoning the cool and reasonable thing.

"My point exactly," Will shot back. "And you know what? Fine. If that's what I have to do to hold this team together, fine. Let's fuck. Let's get it out of the way once and for all. If that's your price, then okay. I'm more than willing to take one for the team—or am I supposed to do you? Whichever is fine by me because unlike you, MacAllister, I —"

With an inarticulate sound, Taylor launched himself at Will, and Will, unprepared, fell back over the log he'd been sitting on, head ringing from Taylor's fist connecting with his jaw. This was rage, not passion, although for one bewildered instant Will's body processed the feel of Taylor's hard, thin, muscular length landing on top of his own body as a good thing—a very good thing.

This was followed by the very bad thing of Taylor trying to knee him in the guts—which sent a new and clearer message to Will's mind and body.

And there was nothing Will would have loved more than to let go and pulverize Taylor, to take him apart, piece by piece, but he didn't forget for an instant—even if Taylor did—how physically vulnerable Taylor still was; so his efforts went into keeping Taylor from injuring himself—which was not easy to do wriggling and rolling around on the uneven ground. Even at 75 percent, Taylor was a significant threat, and Will took a few hits before he managed to wind his arms around the other man's torso, yanking him into a sitting position facing Will, and immobilizing him in a butterfly lock.

Taylor tried a couple of heaves, but he had tired fast. Will was the better wrestler anyway, being taller, broader, and heavier. Taylor relied on speed and surprise; he went in for all kinds of esoteric martial arts, which was fine unless someone like Will got him on the ground. Taylor was usually too smart to let that happen, which just went to show how furious he was.

Will could feel that fury still shaking Taylor—locked in this ugly parody of a lover's embrace. He shook with exhaustion too, breath shuddering in his lungs as he panted into Will's shoulder. His wind was shit these days, his heart banging frantically against Will's. These marks of physical distress undermined Will's own anger, reminding him how recently he had almost lost Taylor for good.

Taylor's moist breath against Will's ear was sending a confusingly erotic message, his body hot and sweaty—but Christ, he was thin. Will could feel—could practically count—ribs, the hard links of spine, the ridges of scapula in Taylor's fleshless back. And it scared him; his hold changed instinctively from lock to hug.

"You crazy bastard," he muttered into Taylor's hair.

Taylor struggled again, and this time Will let him go. Taylor got up, not looking at Will, not speaking, walking unsteadily, but with a peculiar dignity, over to the tent.

Watching him, Will opened his mouth, then shut it. Why the hell would he apologize? Taylor had jumped *him*. He watched, scowling, as Taylor crawled inside the tent, rolled out his sleeping bag onto the air mattress Will had remembered to set up for him, pulled his boots off, and climbed into the bag, pulling the flap over his head—like something going back into its shell.

This is stupid, Will thought. We neither of us want this. But what he said was, "Sweet dreams to you too."

Taylor said nothing.

# ABOUT THE AUTHOR

Author of over sixty titles of classic Male/Male fiction featuring twisty mystery, kickass adventure, and unapologetic man-on-man romance, **JOSH LANYON**'s work has been translated into eleven languages. Her FBI thriller *Fair Game* was the first Male/Male title to be published by Harlequin Mondadori, then the largest romance publisher in Italy. *Stranger on the Shore* (Harper Collins Italia) was the first M/M title to be published in print. In 2016 *Fatal Shadows* placed #5 in Japan's annual Boy Love novel list (the first and only title by a foreign author to place on the list). The Adrien English series was awarded the All Time Favorite Couple by the Goodreads M/M Romance Group.

She is an Eppie Award winner, a four-time Lambda Literary Award finalist (twice for Gay Mystery), an Edgar nominee and the first ever recipient of the Goodreads All Time Favorite M/M Author award.

Josh is married and lives in Southern California.

Find other Josh Lanyon titles at www.joshlanyon.com, and follow her on Twitter, Facebook, Goodreads, Instagram and Tumblr.

For extras and other exclusives, please join Josh on Patreon at https://www.patreon.com/joshlanyon.

# ALSO BY JOSH LANYON

## NOVELS

### The ADRIEN ENGLISH Mysteries

*Fatal Shadows • A Dangerous Thing • The Hell You Say*
*Death of a Pirate King • The Dark Tide*
*So This is Christmas • Stranger Things Have Happened*

### The HOLMES & MORIARITY Mysteries

*Somebody Killed His Editor • All She Wrote*
*The Boy with the Painful Tattoo • In Other Words...Murder*

### The ALL'S FAIR Series

*Fair Game • Fair Play • Fair Chance*

### The ART OF MURDER Series

*The Mermaid Murders •The Monet Murders*
*The Magician Murders*

## OTHER NOVELS

*The Ghost Wore Yellow Socks*
*Mexican Heat (with Laura Baumbach)*
*Strange Fortune • Come Unto These Yellow Sands*
*This Rough Magic • Stranger on the Shore • Winter Kill*
*Murder in Pastel • Jefferson Blythe, Esquire*
*The Curse of the Blue Scarab • Murder Takes the High Road*
*Séance on a Summer's Night • The Ghost Had an Early Check-Out*

# NOVELLAS

## The DANGEROUS GROUND Series

*Dangerous Ground • Old Poison • Blood Heat*
*Dead Run • Kick Start*The I SPY Series
*I Spy Something Bloody • I Spy Something Wicked*
*I Spy Something Christmas*

## The IN A DARK WOOD Series

*In a Dark Wood • The Parting Glass*

## The DARK HORSE Series

*The Dark Horse • The White Knight*

## The DOYLE & SPAIN Series

*Snowball in Hell*

## The HAUNTED HEART Series

*Haunted Heart Winter*

## The XOXO FILES Series

*Mummie Dearest*

# OTHER NOVELLAS

*Cards on the Table • The Dark Farewell • The Darkling Thrush*
*The Dickens with Love • Don't Look Back • A Ghost of a Chance*
*Lovers and Other Strangers • Out of the Blue • A Vintage Affair*
*Lone Star (in Men Under the Mistletoe)*
*Green Glass Beads (in Irregulars)*
*Blood Red Butterfly • Everything I Know • Baby, It's Cold*
*A Case of Christmas • Murder Between the Pages*

## SHORT STORIES

*A Limited Engagement • The French Have a Word for It*

*In Sunshine or In Shadow • Until We Meet Once More*

*Icecapade (in His for the Holidays) • Perfect Day • Heart Trouble*

*In Plain Sight • Wedding Favors • Wizard's Moon*

*Fade to Black • Night Watch • Plenty of Fish*

*The Boy Next Door • Halloween is Murder*

## COLLECTIONS

*Stories (Vol. 1) • Sweet Spot (the Petit Morts)*

*Merry Christmas, Darling (Holiday Codas)*

*Christmas Waltz (Holiday Codas 2)*

*I Spy...Three Novellas*

*Point Blank (Five Dangerous Ground Novellas)*

*Dark Horse, White Knight (Two Novellas)*

*The Adrien English Mysteries*

*The Adrien English Mysteries 2*